MW01100403

THE BOOK SMUGGLERS'

QUARTERLY ALMANAC

This first edition published 2016 by Book Smugglers Publishing
Astoria (USA) & Cambridge (UK)
www.booksmugglerspub.com

Edited by Ana Grilo & Thea James

978-1-942302-36-0 (Ebook)
978-1-942302-35-3 (Paperback)

Illustration © by Kristina Tsenova
Cover Layout by Kenda Montgomery

Book Design and Ebook Conversion by Thea James

So say we all.

Table of Contents

An Introduction

THE BOOK SMUGGLERS

ANOTHER QUARTER, ANOTHER ALMANAC, ANOTHER great opportunity to devour great stories and essays hand-picked by your friendly neighborhood book smugglers. (You're welcome.)

This volume opens with a teaser—Isabel Yap, forthcoming author of the Hurricane Heels series, writes an essay about magical girls and what makes them so special. Spoiler: it's not the cool weapons and flashy powers. Or at least, it's not *only* that. Heroes are heroes because they dare and survive and *endure:* a concept that has permeated our Superhero Season of short stories this summer, and is also true of another entry in this almanac. Susan Jane Bigelow's character Penny Silverwing, previously known as Broken, is now back in an original standalone short story, "Winter's Flight."

Speaking of heroes, one of our personal heroes, Emmy Award winning producer Javier Grillo-Marxuach (of *Lost* fame), wrote an essay about what makes *Star Trek The Motion Picture* an (arguably) enduring treat. Also a treat: Michal Wojcik's "Mrs. Yaga", originally published in 2014 as part of our inaugural season of short stories, now reprinted in this volume. "Mrs. Yaga" not only fits the loose theme of this second Almanac (amazing, powerful women), but also is a quirky, 90s reinterpretation of the Baba Yaga myth.

Have you ever considered if there's a difference in the way men and women write fantasy? The ever-fabulous Kate Elliott navigates this minefield with her trademark skill and brilliance. Meanwhile, comics writer Jim Zub talks about writing the strange side of Tokyo, research for his ongoing comic book series, *Wayward*.

Our second work of original fiction collected in this volume is also the subject of the gorgeous art (by Kristina Tsenova) featured on the cover. We acquired "Ruby" by debut author Anna Hight *especially* for this Almanac. Originally submitted nearly two years ago, "Ruby" is a story that has stayed with us since our first read—it's all about blame, monsters, and empowerment. We hope you fall in love with it, just as much as we did.

Seanan McGuire wrote a fantastic novella called *Every Heart a Doorway* and we loved it so much, we asked the author to write a piece for our ongoing "Where to Start With..." series. In her essay, she talks about the gateway drug of Portal Fantasies. Next up, Yoon Ha Lee, author of the fabulous and best-of-the-year science fiction novel *Ninefox Gambit*, writes an essay titled "Fruitcakes and Gimchi IN SPAAACE." Don't you want to stop reading this intro immediately and flip through to read that, like, right now?

Finally, anchoring the Almanac we have two provocative and thoughtful entries to close out this quarter. The first essay is a piece by Mimi Mondal, a Clarion West Octavia Butler Scholar, and her experience with Harry Potter, race, and the prickly questions of privilege. Last but not least, we have a piece from Tansy Rayner Roberts about the "One Girl" trope on superhero teams.

But wait, we almost forgot! An almanac without reviews? NO WAY. In this volume, Ana reviews optimistic science fiction sequel *Closed and Common Orbit* by Becky Chambers, and Thea reviews YA fantasy novel *The Scourge* from Jennifer A. Nielsen.

We hope you enjoy, and until next time, we remain...

Your Friendly Neighborhood Book Smugglers
September 2016

What Makes A Magical Girl?

ISABEL YAP

WHAT MAKES A MAGICAL GIRL? I think everyone can come up with their own criteria. For me, there are three essential elements:

1. She's not fearless, but she's willing to fight.

2. She loves relentlessly, with an open heart.

3. Her strength comes from authenticity—from being true to herself.

Growing up, the magical girl series that I followed most religiously wasn't *Sailormoon* (I've actually still never watched or read a version of *Sailormoon* beyond the first few episodes). The show that most strongly shaped my ideas of the genre was *Akazukin Chacha.* "Red riding hood" Chacha is a magician-in-training who is kind, cheerful, and awful at casting spells. Her best friends are Riiya, a super strong werewolf boy; and Shiine, a talented young wizard. Together the trio has many slapstick adventures; but when the demon lord Daimao creates monsters that threaten the land's peace, the three friends come together so that Chacha can transform into the magical princess, Holy Up. With love, courage, and hope, the bumbling Chacha harnesses the strength of their friendship, to turn their magical trinkets into weapons that can vanquish enemies with a single strike.

I liked Chacha a lot. She was cute, endlessly optimistic, and a total badass in Holy Up form. Her adventures made me laugh, and she nailed the Magical Girl criteria through several seasons. She fought even when she was scared; she loved her friends and her teacher without limit; and she always remained true to herself. But when *I* was a girl—safe and shielded from many things—I didn't want to *be* Chacha. Or any magical girl. I didn't think I needed that kind of strength.

Oddly enough, my desire to be more like a magical girl—to cling to hope, to be strong enough to fight week after week, to lean on others without shame or fear, and likewise give of myself generously—has grown, and become more urgent, the father away I am from qualifying as a *girl*. And I never feel this desire more strongly than when I am weak, or powerless.

My first corporate intern ship, I was bright-eyed and eager to please. I liked my role. I was excited to do my work and contribute a lot to the team. I happily struck up conversations with other interns and full-time employees. I figured that although this was tech, and male employees far outnumbered female ones, this was *also* the Bay Area and modern days. Things would be *fine*.

Yeah, I was naïve. I learned quickly that it was stupid of me to give my number out, and expect that person to text me only in a professional context. Bonding over a shared cultural background could apparently be an invitation to unwanted advances. It was not okay for me to decline any offers of help lest I wish to be bombarded by confessions of longing and devil emoji on Skype. And what I hoped would be a networking conversation about career goals would devolve into a chat about whether I had a boyfriend, if I would wear a kimono and pose for pictures, and if I wanted to sniff the sauce spilled on someone's pants.

Towards the end of my internship I stopped working at my desk because I felt so uncomfortable. All those instances were with different people, and it was exhausting. I couldn't really process at the time what was happening, or why. Now I know—it was harassment, and I was encountering it for the first time. I didn't know how to deal with it.

I do remember that every woman I asked for advice told me: *this happens. You need to toughen up and be prepared for it.*

Going through that was the first time I genuinely wished for magical girl powers. Something to take care of the creeps when they approached. Something to keep me shielded from them, and keep them away from other women. Something that would let me stop being afraid, and tense, and guarded all the time. I'd lost whatever it was—that shoujo sparkle, that gutsy courage. Could I ever get it back?

It's been a few years since, and as it stands, my answer is: yes. But not quite in the way I expected. Because the more I've grown up, the more I've realized: magical girl stories aren't about superpowered beings who go through life in a happy haze of always winning. They are stories about *growing up*. About facing suffering and defeat, and learning from life. About losing an ordinary existence—and yes, a lot of innocence—to gain the strength to fight.

They're about becoming more *fully* one's self—all shades of it, even the difficult, ugly parts that are terrifying to face. And they are about finding true friends—forever friends. The kind who will stick with you and make you stronger, who will watch you transform and cheer you on, who will see you possessed with evil and won't give up on you. Magical girls don't go it alone. I'm thinking of Homura and Madoka; Usagi and the Sailor Senshi; Sakura and Tomoe; Mako and Ryuko; Riiya, Shiine, and Chacha. And I'm thinking of all the friends I've had the pleasure of knowing, loving, and drawing strength from, through the years.

I wrote *Hurricane Heels* because I wanted to write a story filled with girls that *I knew*—and extend the magical girl mythos beyond just teenagers, because there are much older girls going through this same journey. Flawed girls trying to survive in an insane, hostile world— but still one worth saving, worth living in. I wrote to bring their scars to life. And in doing so, I realized: what makes a magical girl isn't an overabundance of frills, extreme weaponry, or kawaii blasts of doom (though these can all, of course, help). It's the inner qualities and strength, shining (sparkling?) through—and we can, each of us, draw on that ourselves, and save the world: battle heels optional.

Winter's Flight

SUSAN JANE BIGELOW

NEW YORK HAD FROZEN. PENNY Silverwing looked out over the city, her breath coming out in white puffs, as she hovered inches above the roof of the abandoned hotel on the Greenpoint waterfront where she lived. The sun was beginning to set; soon it would be gone entirely and another frigid night would begin.

The cold settled deep in her bones. When she'd first lived on the streets decades ago, the winters in New York had been much warmer. Now that climate controls had had finally cooled a dangerously chaotic, warming planet it was nearly unbearable.

Once the sun set she'd be able to fly. She had contraband to deliver: drugs, weapons, books, that sort of thing. There were people who paid good money for someone who could dart high above the clouds where no one was looking. They weren't exactly good people, but the work kept her in food and battery charges for her tiny underpowered space heater.

The gig also let her stay in New York without running afoul of the CMP. Liesl Palekar and other people in that government's security services might still be out there looking for her. Penny couldn't apply for a real job, or any kind of government assistance, without tripping a dozen alarms.

Most importantly, flying deliveries let her stay near her son, Amos.

Her eyes left the sun setting over the low buildings of Manhattan, just across the frozen East River, and focused on the skyscrapers of Queens rising to the northeast. Beyond that was Amos, living in a warm, friendly little house with his adoptive parents.

He would be getting home from school, now. He was fourteen, so close to being grown, and he looked more like his father, Sky Ranger, every day.

Penny had never worked up the courage to talk to him. She had no idea how to start. What could she possibly say that would make up for thirteen stolen years? She wasn't even sure he knew he was adopted.

Penny sighed as the light dwindled and street lights flickered on below. She looked out at the western horizon again—

—and saw a human form flying high above the city.

"Hey!" she yelped, leaping into the air without stopping to think. She streaked after them, every muscle straining, every ounce of energy channeled into flight. Her long silver hair whipped out behind her and the wind tore at her face as she rocketed across the river and over the grid of Manhattan, eyes fixed on the point where she'd seen that single flying form.

But when she arrived, they were already gone. She looked wildly around, the icy air snatching at her breath.

"Hey!" she called again. "I saw you! It's okay! I won't hurt you! Come back!

"Come back, Sky!" she screamed into the wind. "Come back!"

She darted from building to building, taking extra care not to be seen. She'd been foolish to fly while it was still light out. People looked up, sometimes. Sensors couldn't see her if she stayed below the line of the buildings, but people weren't so easy to fool. There hadn't been extrahumans over this city since Union Tower fell, they'd talk. That could bring the military down on her again. She wasn't sure she could take them without Dee by her side.

Doubt crept in. Had it been a trick of the light? Maybe she'd seen what she wanted to see and nothing more.

She landed on a roof and sat, feeling inept and hopeless.

Somewhere in the past year, ever since she'd launched herself at a CMP chopper in First Landing and been blown into a million pieces, her confidence had shattered.

But she was so sure. She *had* seen someone soaring in the air above.

It couldn't be... *him*. He was imprisoned on Tragela. Right?

The only other extrahumans she knew who were free and could fly were Emily, Torres, and Jill. Jill could barely get off the ground, so it wasn't her. She couldn't imagine Emily coming here; at least not anymore. Whatever little spark for adventure she had, the CMP bombing of Mandolia had extinguished it. Penny hoped it wasn't for good.

Torres, then? Maybe.

If so, then something had to be wrong. The time and expense it would take for the Order of St. Val to covertly shuttle an extrahuman to Earth from Valen had been astronomical when they'd done it for Dee and Penny a year before.

Penny dared peek her head up above the line of the buildings and scanned the horizon. All she could see were the lights of the city and suburbs stretching off into the west.

Dee would know. Dee had connections to West Arve Temple, the Order, and that shit, Prelate Celeste. Penny ground her teeth. She hated to go hat in hand to the Order after they'd stolen her son away—no matter their reasons. She also wasn't sure how she'd approach Dee after not having seen or spoken

23

to her in a year. But she'd so it; otherwise she knew she would fixate on this and accomplish nothing.

But what do you have to do here in New York anyway?

Penny ignored the voice. She would finish her deliveries for the night, go back to the hotel, and sleep. Tomorrow she would find Dee and sort all this out.

Penny dreamed of flying with Sky Ranger, but not the Sky she'd known all those years ago. This Sky Ranger was older, his eyes full of nightmares she could only guess at, and no matter how fast she flew he was always just out of reach.

"Fine!" she shouted at his receding form. "Why did I bother chasing you anyway?"

But when she turned around to fly away, there he was. He was always there, no matter what she did.

When she woke to the stale air and darkness of the hotel room, she whimpered with relief. *Please don't let him be back,* she thought. *I don't think I can stand it.*

Penny's contacts in the courier business had actually paid her, for once, so she went out and picked up a few things: food, a month's charge for the space heater's batteries, a new pair of shapeless sweatpants, and a warm pullover with a hood. Penny had never gotten out of the habit of living with as little as possible.

However, on impulse, she picked up a pair of binoculars. Maybe they'd do her some good.

She took the bus to the far side of Queens, not wanting to risk flying in daylight, and hung around on the corner near Amos's house. She bought a coffee and sat on a bench outside the local Reform Party office, watching the members in their neatly-pressed uniforms and caps with black-and-white insignia come and go. The caps were new. When had they started doing that?

Their eyes slid right over her. She was just another unkempt middle-aged woman in a city full of them. She was no threat. She was nobody at all. Penny sighed, feeling all of her forty-eight years weighing her down.

And then Amos walked by.

She perked up, watching him with his friends; she didn't know their names. Tall boy. Laughing boy. There was a girl this time, too—someone Penny had never seen. Amos was grinning, listening to some tale the tall boy was spinning.

He is so beautiful.

Amos's gaze fell on her for an instant, and she froze in terror. His eyes reminded her of her own, and she opened her mouth, as if to speak. There was a question on his face. He recognized her, maybe. She'd been sitting here, watching him, for the better part of a year now.

Penny almost said something, but the words wouldn't come. She couldn't think of anything at all to say that could bridge this gap. She couldn't think of a way to make him see her, really *see* her, instead of looking her way and seeing a wreck of a person sitting on concrete.

The moment passed. He looked back to his friends, and they laughed their way down the street, away from the Reform Party office, away from Penny on her bench.

She felt like a creep and a coward, just like every other time. Her heart froze, just a little bit more.

After a long while she finished the last of the coffee and made her slow, stumbling way towards the subway.

The little missionary outpost of the Order of St. Val was in one of the worst parts of the Upper East Side. It was in a neighborhood that Penny knew well from when she'd lived on the streets of New York.

She emerged from the subway onto achingly familiar streets and was twenty-five again: homeless again, hopeless again, Broken again. The place looked, felt, and *smelled* the same, even after all this time.

She looked around, thinking maybe she'd spot the place where Michael Forward had first found her, bearing a baby, a quest, and a prophecy. Her life had changed in that moment, though she had no idea of it then.

That place had to be near here, right? Would she even be able to tell? Those years were all a blur of sameness, sadness, terror, hunger, cold, and yearning. The streets were familiar, but she couldn't remember exactly where she'd been. Was it… there? Or down there? Or…?

No. She couldn't get lost in the past again. She knew herself too well; the past would drive its nails into her if she let it. Penny—*not* Broken—forced herself into the present, and hobbled down the avenue towards the building containing the mission.

"Yes, I know you," the cheery-faced woman in blue at the front desk said. "I'm Bernice. I was on the flight here from Valen with you."

"Sure, I remember," said Penny, though she didn't. "I'm looking for Dee. She around?"

"Ah," said Bernice, frowning. "Well, unfortunately Dee is… no longer here, I'm afraid."

"What?" said Penny, startled. "You're kidding. She left? Where did she go?"

Bernice paused, giving Penny an appraising stare. It occurred to Penny that she hadn't bothered to brush her hair in well over a week. "I remember that you were her friend. I'm surprised she didn't tell you herself."

"We've been out of touch," Penny said, trying not to let herself sound too pathetic. "Do you know where she went or not?"

Bernice crossed her arms over her chest. "She's not here. That's all I can tell you."

"Please," insisted Penny. "It's important. I think something's wrong. I'm sorry I wasn't in touch, but I need to talk to her. You know who I am, so please tell me: will she be coming back? Did anyone else come from Valen?"

Bernice pursed her lips, then relented. "Fine, then, if you must know Dee went to look for what's left of her family in Connecticut. And then she was going to go back to Valen. That's a tricky thing. But Prelate Celeste set it up, and... We will miss her. We already do, she was such a help to us."

Celeste. Penny bristled at the name. Prelate Celeste of West Arve Temple back on Valen had been responsible for what had happened to Amos, and for so much more. "Helped? How?"

"Things have settled down a little in the past year," said Bernice. "There's something going on in the government and everything's loosened up. Travel is becoming possible again. Dee won't be coming back here, she has other places to be. And no, no one else has come."

"You're sure?"

"As sure as I can be," Bernice said. Worry passed across her face. "Penny? What's this all about?"

But Penny was already out the door.

She sat atop her hotel roof again, staring out at the waning light of the day. She scanned the horizon near where she'd seen—or thought she'd seen—the other flyer yesterday.

Nothing.

The light was a lmost gone when she thought she spied a pinprick hovering above the southern part of Manhattan. She grabbed the binoculars and tried to zero in on it.

Yes. *Yes.* A human form, glimpsed only for an instant, darting between buildings.

A dark-skinned woman with short-cropped white hair.

Penny lowered the binoculars, heart pounding. She didn't know her.

This was someone new.

She was in the air before she could think. Penny streaked over the East River and toward the heart of Manhattan. She didn't care that it was still light. She didn't care who saw. Let the Confederation come for her. They'd tried and failed so many times before.

Penny touched down on one of the buildings she'd seen the other flying woman and looked wildly around. "Where are you?" she cried into the wind and darkening sky. "Come out! I'm safe! I won't—"

Penny caught herself in a sudden moment of clarity. Here she was, standing unsteadily atop a building in New York, *New York* of all places, hollering at the top of her lungs that she was *safe.*

There was a soft *whoosh*ing sound, and Penny looked up, thinking she might see police or CMP hoppers, but instead she saw a tiny, elderly woman floating above her, mouth drawn down into a frown.

"You should go away," she said in lightly accented English. "Don't ever come looking for me again. Leave this city before I can no longer cover for you."

"Wait," said Penny. "Who are you? You fly! So—so do I."

The old woman crossed her arms over her slight chest. "I know. And?"

Penny was at a loss for what to say. "And… it's been so long since I met someone new. There's so few of us left."

"That's a good thing," snapped the old woman. "Go. Don't fly. Take the train like a regular person. Don't fly again here. I know who you're working for, those criminals who have you flying courier for them. They're bad at keeping secrets. Got it?"

Penny felt about ten years old again, and on the business end of a dressing down by Triad or Brick, the two who took care of the children back at the old Union. But she held her ground. "You don't even know who I am."

"I know plenty. Silverwing. You were in the Union with *him*. I remember you." She glowered at Penny. "Long time ago, you and the rest of your thugs came knocking at my door. If you'd caught me, I'd have gone to that jail you called a home, and I would have died with everyone else when it came down. Now go away and leave me in peace."

With that, the woman turned and slipped into the shadows between darkened buildings, and was gone.

Penny rode the train home like a regular person. She sifted through the conversation again and again, trying to understand.

The old woman had obviously been an unregistered extrahuman, back during the old days when the Extrahuman Union was up and running and the Law Enforcement Division had hunted people like her down. That was depressingly clear.

Leave this city before I can no longer cover for you.

Penny didn't want to think about what that meant, but rebellious understanding came anyway. People had seen her and reported it to the authorities, and this old woman had tried to cover it up somehow.

But why? More unsettlingly, how? Did she work for the government? Was she a Reformist, or, worse, a CMP agent?

That settled a few things, though. She wouldn't be able to keep flying deliveries for her untrustworthy employers. For all she knew, they'd turned her in themselves. Maybe she could do something else.

Or maybe she should take the old woman's advice and leave. Dee had already gone. What was there for her here, now, anyway? It had been a year and she still hadn't even talked to her son. She had only ever watched him walk by.

And… if she was honest, this wasn't her city anymore. She'd been off-planet for nearly two decades. The New York she'd known first as a child and young woman in the Extrahuman Union and then as a homeless escapee had sunk down into the mud of the rivers and the sea, and a new one had been built on top of the ruins.

Penny Silverwing felt old, then, for the first time in her life.

The next day she stayed by the window in her abandoned hotel, peering out at the buildings and streets below. People moved past, either alone, in pairs, or in groups. They all seemed to have somewhere to go, somewhere to be.

An awful, vicious, all-consuming sadness nipped at her— the old depression, she thought. Hello, my friend. It's been a long time.

She was as good as homeless, again, in New York. She lived in an abandoned building, fending for herself, hiding out and alone and hated. Time had become a snake turning to sink its fangs in her. She sighed, and lay on the bed, the outside world forgotten.

Penny didn't do any deliveries for her clients that night, and a few of them left some very angry messages. One or two made some not-so-veiled threats.

Let them come, she thought, still feeling the pull of depression. She could handle it. They could only kill her. She would just come back anyway.

But they didn't come. Maybe they knew better. Maybe they'd been warned off. Or maybe she was just lucky, for once.

Penny dreamed of flying unfettered through empty skies that night, and woke felt a little better. The sun had come up after all, and her heart was filled with an unfamiliar sort of hope. Maybe today she could act.

She ate, pulled her hair into a ratty-looking bun, and jammed a wool cap over it. There. She looked different enough that someone looking for her probably wouldn't recognize her at first glance.

She took the train to downtown Queens and made her way to the park where Union Tower had once stood. The last time she'd been here, CMP Captain Liesl Palekar had set up a trap for her and Dee. But this time there was no Palekar, no snipers, nothing. There was only a rush of crowds and the hum of electric vehicles whipping by.

There was a bench near where she was pretty certain the tower entrance had been. She sat in it, looking at the empty space where she'd spent her childhood. Where so many friends had died the day the Confederation had blown the tower up. She clenched her fists, trying to fight the wave of emotion.

"I thought I'd find you here," a voice said. Penny started out of her reverie, expecting to see Palekar, come to find her at last, but it was the old woman instead. She looked smaller in daylight, and much frailer. On the ground she couldn't be more than half Penny's height.

"May I sit?" she asked.

Penny nodded mutely.

"Thank you." She sat. "I was hard on you last night. I'm not sorry for it. What your people did long ago was… very, very wrong."

"I know," Penny said softly. "I'm sorry for it."

The old woman waved her hand. "Sorry doesn't change the past. But… what's done is done. So. It was here. The prison."

"It wasn't a prison," said Penny.

"That's why you escaped it, then?" Penny gave the woman a hard look. "I read your file," the old woman said with a humorless smile.

"My file," Penny's worst suspicions were right, then. "A CMP file?"

"No. Regular police. They have files on everybody." The elderly woman shook her head. "For what it's worth, I was sorry when this happened." She gestured at the empty space where the tower had stood. "Despite all the evil this place produced."

"They took us as children," Penny said, trying not to let her sudden fury show. "They raised us. I was just a little *girl* when they took me. I didn't remember my parents or even my own name for years!"

The old woman held up a hand. "I know. Forgive me. It's hard to let go of an old fight."

"We did what we had to do to survive."

"Did you?" She arched an eyebrow at Penny. "Now you sound like *him*. Like your last Sky Ranger."

"Maybe he had a point," Penny shot back, trying not to think about Sky. "And you're one to talk. How did you get to see police files anyway? How are you 'covering' for me? Who do you work for?"

The old woman grunted a laugh. "I don't work for anyone. I… have an arrangement. I do services for the police. I track people. I give them some of my blood for testing. It lets me stay free and alive, and they leave me alone so I can help people who need it." She glared at Penny. "Another of those services is letting them know if any of *you* ever returned."

Penny started to say something, but the old woman held up her hand again.

"I didn't," she said. "Not this time. I should have, I know. But I didn't."

"Why not? You don't know me."

"Like I said," the other extrahuman sighed. "I do know you. And maybe this is a way for me to make peace with the past."

Penny nodded, thinking of Amos. "I get that."

"Good. Now. Will you leave?"

Penny was about to agree when movement caught her eye. There were more police here than she'd expected.

A *lot* more. And some of those uniforms were CMP gray.

"You liar! You set me up!" Penny hissed. The old woman's eyes went wide with shock.

"She spotted us! Fire, now!" a harsh male voice cried.

Penny leaped up into the air as guns exploded around her. Tranquilizer darts and bullets missed her by millimeters. She could hear people screaming on the ground as she rocketed into the gap between nearby buildings.

She looked back only long enough to see them tackle the old woman to the ground, handcuffs at the ready.

They'd sent hoppers, of course. Penny spent the rest of the day losing the light, maneuverable aircraft in the warren of the city. She blasted through subway tunnels, between buildings, and through the clouds. At last they gave up, and she could breathe again.

She didn't dare return to the hotel, not after all this. She had no way of knowing whether they knew where she'd been holed up. She also couldn't possibly know if they were tracking her in some other way, like through her transit card.

So she made her slow way through the city on foot—or, in her case, by moving her legs to approximate walking while she hovered a micron off the ground. It usually fooled people, and she had no energy to actually walk tonight.

At last she was too exhausted. She sat under a bridge, hunger rumbling in her belly and cold seeping into her bones.

She was grounded. She had nowhere to go. Dee was gone. The Order's mission was far away, and the government was looking for her.

Penny burrowed into a hollow out of view of the street, wrapped her coat tight around her, jammed her freezing hands into her pockets, and slept.

The sun shone high above and Broken was picking through trash behind an apartment building. Food was here sometimes. She glanced skyward, thinking maybe she'd seen the shadow of someone flying up there. Sky Ranger? Someone else? What did it matter, though? Broken couldn't fly. She hadn't been able to fly for years. Her attention wandered, then she started picking through the trash again.

Penny watched her—maybe Broken felt Penny watching. Their eyes met.

"I hate you," said Penny softly.

Broken shrugged. "You are me."

There was a soft *whoosh* of air and Silverwyng deftly landed near them. "Hello!" she chirped. "Do... I know you?"

Broken winced and looked away.

"Get lost," sighed Penny. "I don't need another one of us here."

"Are you sisters? I can't tell you apart," Silverwyng said.

Penny looked at herself through Silverwyng's eyes and knew she looked very similar to her younger, homeless, broken self. But she also knew Silverwyng was lying.

"You know who we are," said Penny.

Silverwyng shook her head, not wanting to believe. "It shouldn't have been this way."

"Leave me alone," groused Broken. "I don't want anything to do with any of you."

"You're over," said Penny. "You don't exist. Either of you! I outlived you both."

"And yet here we are," Broken laughed, but there was no joy in the sound.

"Don't you have something to do?" Silverwyng asked Penny.

"Unfinished business," mumbled Broken. "Gotta do the right thing when you can."

Penny felt her mouth go dry. "I can't."

Broken sighed. Silverwyng shook her head.

"Crimson Cadet says you have to have a strong moral center," Silverwyng said.

Broken paused. "Michael believes that, too," she said softly.

Penny closed her eyes. "Damn it."

When she opened her eyes again Silverwyng was gone. But Broken remained.

"Why didn't you disappear with her?" Penny demanded. "Why don't you just go away! I'm not you! Not anymore! I never want to think about you again! I don't—I can't be you anymore!"

Broken looked away, but there were tears on her face.

"Forgive me," one, or both, of them whispered, and the dream fell apart.

She awoke to an unexpected thaw. The sun shone brightly above; the weather had shifted. The wind had died down to a pleasant breeze. It wasn't warm, not exactly, but it wasn't freezing either.

Spring? Maybe. She'd lost track of the seasons.

The dream returned to her in all its vividness, and she clenched her fists again.

She wasn't Broken. And she wasn't Silverwyng.

And yet… Penny was both of them, and more. The fresh air of Valen was still in her nostrils, the song of the fish and the light of the trees of Mandolia. She was Dee and Emily and Jill and Sky Ranger, she was James and Janeane and Renna, she was the possibility of Ban Delarian and the memory of Michael Forward.

Penny was herself.

She felt the fog of hopelessness lifting, and she could think clearly again.

They'd been taking the old extrahuman woman into custody as she left. It had been a trap for her as much as it had been for Penny. Maybe covering for her had been the last straw, who knew? They'd likely be holding her at the CMP regional office in a skyscraper in Queens.

Penny wasn't Dee—she couldn't just go in there and blast the place. She'd just have to do this her way.

She lifted off the ground, unafraid, and soared through the bright and sunny skies of Manhattan towards Queens.

Night.

The skyscraper with the CMP logo emblazoned on its side stretched up into the sky. Gray hoppers flew lazily past.

Penny thought of Jill, who used her limited flight powers to break into places she shouldn't be. She'd studied this place all day, and she was pretty sure the prisoners would be on the nineteenth floor. The windows were reinforced.

But the twentieth floor… that was another story.

The Confederation Military Police were smart—they'd put high fences around the building. But even though they held an extrahuman in custody, they still didn't think in three dimensions, and were lazily overconfident. Maybe Bernice was right, maybe things were slipping somehow.

And… there. Someone had left a window cracked to catch some of the lingering warmth of the first nice day in months. New Yorkers didn't change.

Penny silently lifted off from the roof of the building across the street and crossed the gap in a swift instant, unseen by the hoppers. She opened the window, gently pushed the screen aside, and slipped in.

The office was empty. It looked like any other place, except for CMP regalia and memorabilia scattered around everywhere.

In fact, this looked like it might be some kind of medical section. There were anatomy diagrams on the wall, and what looked like some kind of medical tech on the desks. The CMP always had tech that was way ahead of the crap they let the general public have. But that also made them overconfident. Penny slipped out of the office into the darkened corridor.

There were rooms with patients in beds lining the corridor. Penny didn't want to know what kinds of things they were hooked up to. The doors were all closed, except for one. Penny returned to the office and grabbed a heavy model of a CMP ship and crept up on the square of light from the open door.

A doctor was inside, making notes on a tablet. His back was turned. Penny floated as close as she dared, then brained him with the ship model. He went down easy, bleeding from a gash on the back of his head. She turned him over, placed her foot on his neck and pushed down.

"Don't do anything," she said softly as his eyes bugged out. "I need to get to the level below. Gotta friend there. I can kill you now if you'd rather. I've killed people before. I don't mind doing it."

He gurgled and she lifted the boot ever so slightly. "Two dozen soldiers down there," he gasped. "They'll shoot you on sight!"

"Then maybe you can help me," she said icily. "This woman is old and she flies. Which cell is she in?" She ground her boot into his windpipe.

His eyes widened. "She's here!" he gasped when she let up. "This-this level. I swear! I'll take you!"

She rifled through his pockets and found his small sidearm. He seemed to wilt a little at that. She flew backwards and let him get to his feet. She pointed the weapon at him.

"You can't get out of here," he said, rubbing his throat. "There are cameras everywhere. They'll see you."

"Where is she?" demanded Penny.

"Two doors down," he said.

"Show me." As they left the room, she risked a glance at the patient in the bed.

It was Liesl Palekar, the CMP captain who had failed to capture her on Mandolia and then again here in New York. She was hooked up to dozens of wires, tubes, and what looked like… machine parts?

Liesel regarded Penny with eyes that weren't human anymore.

Penny felt a chill go up her spine, and quickly left the room.

The doctor led her down the hall. "They'll be here any minute," he said.

"You said that a minute ago," Penny snapped as he fumbled with the keypad. "Hurry."

The door slid open. Inside, the old extrahuman lay in a medical bed. She looked groggy.

"You," she whispered. "You…?"

Penny crossed the room to her in an instant, and began disconnecting her from the medical gear. "Can you fly?"

The old woman shook her head no. "Some sort of… medicine…"

"They got me with that one, too," Penny said. "It sucks. Come on. Let's get out of here."

"How?"

"You'll have to ride me!" She grabbed the woman to a yelp of protest. Penny winced; she'd apologize later. "Get on my back!"

Alarms blared. Shit. She'd forgotten about the doctor; he'd made his escape and hit the panic button.

"We're going!" cried Penny, grabbing on to the old woman and flying out of the room. "Stop!" cried voices at the end of the hall. Weapons fired, Penny zipped into the office with the window just in time.

But the window had closed. Some kind of automatic locking system.

"Head down!" ordered Penny, extending a fist. She built up speed and rocketed right at it.

The window shattered as she burst through it, tearing open her face and scalp, lacerating her hands and arms. She felt dizzy, and started plunging downward as the world faded to black static.

"Silverwing!" screamed the old woman. "Pull up! Now!"

Penny felt the pain of recovery as her wounds started to knit together, and braked. She pulled up just in time to avoid becoming street pizza and shot off into the night, pursued by hoppers.

They were on a beach somewhere on the northern shore of Long Island Sound. They'd lost the hoppers in a suburban subdivision with a conveniently abandoned underground shopping center, and now they were absolutely, utterly alone.

"I feel a little better now," the old woman said. "Thank you."

"Sure," said Penny. She scratched her head where the blood had caked into her hair. "No trouble."

"I didn't know they were coming, you know. I had no idea."

"I know."

They sat in strained silence for a long moment.

"Sorry about all this," Penny said. "It wouldn't have happened if I'd stayed careful."

The old woman shrugged. "My agreement with them was bound to fail sooner or later. I'm getting too old to be of much use. And I don't think they liked the idea of me helping you."

"But you can't go back, now. Can you?"

The old woman grinned. "To my city? My neighborhood? They won't stop me. I have good friends who will help. I've done a lot of favors for people over the years. You're not the only one who can be a hero, you know."

"I don't doubt it," said Penny, grinning back.

"And what will you do?"

"I… have unfinished business here," Penny said. "I may stay a little while longer."

"Ah. Best we stay on our respective sides of the East River, then."

"Yeah. Agreed."

The old woman stuck out a hand. "I'm Nena."

"Penny."

They shook hands.

"You're right," Nena said. Her smile made the sun come out. "It's nice to meet someone new."

Penny found a different hotel to crash in; this one was only half-built and farther away, out in Nassau County, but it was something. She made some money fixing things for people; she was always good at tinkering. Other than that, she scavenged and foraged. She'd always been good at that, too.

She didn't see much of the CMP after that, but she stayed away from her old haunts just in case.

Then, as spring turned to summer, she went back to Queens and sat on that same street corner to wait. She'd dressed in her nicest clothes, and her hair was as neat as she could make it.

There he came. He was alone, this time.

Before she could talk herself out of it, she fell in step beside him. She felt warm and bright today. Most of all, she felt human and real.

He stopped, and they looked at one another for a long moment.

Penny opened her mouth, and waited for the future to come tumbling out.

Sympathy for The Motion Sickness

JAVIER GRILLO-
MARXUACH

WHEN I WAS YOUNG-ER, AND far more willing to throw things I didn't fully understand under the bus to score points in arguments about the merits of sci-fi franchises, I would call *Star Trek: The Motion Picture* "Star Trek: The Motion Sickness."

I know—HILARIOUS—right?

However, as I continue to careen down the wormhole of not-so dignified-middle-age, I have come to appreciate *Star Trek: The Motion Picture* more and more. Though the reason for my appreciation can certainly be blamed in part for its connection to my childhood and its place in a pop culture body of work I have loved for decades, a lot of it has to do with a growing awareness of everything that *Star Trek: The Motion Picture* is not.

The case against *The Motion Picture* (heretofore shortened to TMP) has been made repeatedly. Detractors call it a ponderous, nigh-plotless dirge in which characters who were perfectly entertaining on television were bled of all their vitality and humor in an attempt to project gravitas. Even at the time of its release, the film's title's postscript "The Motion Picture" felt like a pretentious sigil of these flaws: especially since, only a year earlier, Superman, that most iconic of American pop-cultural symbols, settled for the significantly cuddlier

43

(and more promising-of-fun) "The Movie."

After seeing TMP several times after its release, I eventually resolved to consign it to memory during a time when I was busily distancing myself from many of the things I loved in childhood. I even wrote an essay called "My Year Without *Star Wars*" to explain why this was necessary. However—as time wore on—I figured that an evening spent revisiting the risible and bloated spectacle whose only redeeming value for me had become that it only failed badly enough to beget *Star Trek II: The Wrath of Khan* would be something approximating a good time.

I would be remiss if I didn't mention at this point that, in preparation for this, I devoured a pot brownie the size of which can only be described as monolithic.

As a syrupy cannabinoid fog descended upon my brain, I fired up my DVD of the "Special Director's Edition" of TMP and pressed play. In a minute, my living room filled with the high romance of Jerry Goldsmith's overture.

That's right. As if the film's title didn't already promise a lengthy spell of portentous tedium, TMP would also be the last film for almost two decades released with an *overture*: signifying for all within earshot that this was not merely a spinoff of a television show widely mocked for low production values and an over-emoting lead actor, but rather a Cultural Event on par with the reincarnation of David Lean by way of Stanley Kubrick.

That's when I heard a voice from another room.

"What is that music? It's BEAUTIFUL!"

My fiancée.

Now, my preference when in an altered state of consciousness is to be left alone with my thoughts... especially since, once I have eaten a pot brownie, I usually undergo a physical transformation and become a very shy and slovenly giant panda.

However, I was so shocked by my non-genre-fan-wife-to-be's very honest and visceral reaction to Goldsmith's music that, when she came into the room and sat next to me—telling me that she had never seen TMP—I not only welcomed her to join me in my ursine state, but also did nothing to warn her of what was to come.

What followed was, at the very least, the most fun viewing of TMP that I have ever experienced.

Watching this film in a high-definition monitor with an upscaling DVD player, my fiancée and I were struck by several things. One, most of the cast was in dire need of dance belts. The far-too-tight and pajama-like uniforms provide way more shapes, outlines, and suspicious shadows than a general audience should have to see.

Two, the make-up in this film was clearly not designed for the level of scrutiny possible in the digital viewing environment. Most of the cast members, especially Spock, come across as spackled, painted, shellacked, and... a bit... well... for lack of a better word... queeny.

This may sound harsh, but once someone has pointed out to you that Leonard Nimoy's Spock make-up makes him look more like Faye Dunaway in Mommie Dearest than the incarnation of the character seen in the original TV series, it becomes extremely hard to see anything else.

Three, while we are on the topic of High Camp and melodrama—the film is so full of earnest and loudly declaimed declarations of shoulder-clutching masculine affection ("Dammit, Bones... I NEED you! BADLY!") that, especially in light of the first two items on this list, it is nigh-impossible not to project on the narrative a homoerotic subtext so overwhelming that I began to wonder whether Gore Vidal was hired to do a script rewrite and made trolling the hetero establishment his mission (as he famously admitted to doing with William Wyler's *Ben-Hur*).

These three factors taken into account, *Star Trek: The Motion Picture* rapidly became for us a Douglas Sirkian fever-dream telenovela in which Admiral Kirk once had love affairs—and amicable breakups—with Scotty, Sulu, Chekhov, McCoy, and Spock, but his most recent lover, Commander Decker, knew nothing of it until the Admiral's surprise arrival on the Enterprise, causing much hissing and rending of garments among all involved.

If you ever find yourself stoned out of your ever-loving capacity for reason—and in need of an evening of freely-interpretative reconsideration of an antiquated film—try watching TMP under this assumption. Every one of Spock's eyebrow-cocking reactions, every long, pining look between these heavily made-up, tightly pant-suited men, and every physical instance of manly fellowship will open into a previously undiscovered country of unspoken sexual desire.

While I remember that night as a pivotal moment of bonding between me and my now-wife—and the impressions I relayed above are a reliable part of my comedic repertoire—the inciting incident for it remains etched in my memory and is the cornerstone of my increasing affection for TMP... my wife's reaction to Jerry Goldsmith's overture:

"It's BEAUTIFUL."

In the thirty-seven years since the release of TMP, there have been five additional films starring the original cast, four television series set in the Star Trek universe (with a fifth one—*Star Trek: Discovery*—on the way as of this writing), three feature film sequels to The Next Generation television series, and three films set in the "Kelvin Timeline" (the name given by the Paramount Studios to the alternate universe established by J.J. Abrams and company in their 2009 reboot of the Star Trek franchise).

Not one of them has made me believe that there is beauty in the Star Trek universe.

All these different Star Treks reflect their respective times, and the evolution of the mainstream of taste in popular entertainment: a taste which, in many ways (not the least of which is in the portrayal of ethnically-diverse casts and characters), Star Trek has helped define. However, one franchise alone, no matter how popular and pervasive—and how noble its aims—cannot remain static in the face of taste and culture.

In recent years, Star Trek has become as jacked-up, blown-up, and turned-up as every other popular entertainment (something I began to notice around the time someone decided that *Star Trek: Nemesis* needed to bring some much-needed off-road ATV racing to the franchise). While I have as much of a desire to have my senses overloaded by entertainment that is jacked-up, blown-up, and turned-up as the next guy, the word "beautiful" is seldom the one that comes up in apropos of entertainment that is jacked-up, blown-up, and turned-up.

In the time since that fateful night with the wife and the marijuana brownie, I have periodically revisited TMP with newfound and growing affection for a number of reasons. None of them drug-related. One is that its slow, stately pace does, in fact, allow the viewer to appreciate a great number of moments of artistry that are, inarguably, beautiful.

First and foremost there is Jerry Goldsmith's Academy Award-nominated score. While writing a defense of Jerry Goldsmith is like writing an apology for oxygen—simultaneously obvious yet well out of my weight category—I will say this: listening to Goldsmith, I always get the sense that I'm in the hands of a composer who could easily write John Williams as well as

John Williams, but chose not to for the sake of having bigger fish to fry.

Don't believe me? Listen to the "*The Calling/The Neighborhood*"—the second track of the soundtrack for *Poltergeist* (a film regarded by most genre lovers as the evil, and significantly more entertaining, twin of Spielberg's *E.T.*). In less than five minutes, Goldsmith—with the steady and unpretentious hand of a prolific craftsman who habitually forgets more moves than comprise the repertoire of his peers—pastiches, parodies, and then out-Williams Williams before propelling himself into a sonic universe of his own invention.

For TMP, Goldsmith not only brought his mainstream Hollywood A-game (rightfully influenced by Williams' genre-defining work on Star Wars as well as Maurice Jarre in his sweepingest Lawrence of Arabia idiom) but also the experimental side that led him to pioneering work on films such as *Planet of the Apes*, *The Omen* and *Alien*;

some of the first mainstream films to feature not only ethnic instruments and percussion, but also avant-garde influenced choral work, and electronic experimentation in concert with traditional orchestral techniques.

Like so much of what is artistically great about Star Trek in general, Goldsmith's score for TMP is often given short shrift simply because it exists in service of a science fiction franchise from the time before geek became chic—and because the main title theme went on to become (in a sped-up and abridged version) the main title for all Star Trek for the next twenty years. If nothing else I write here compels you to revisit this film, consider spending two minutes and change listening to the *overture* alone.

If you don't find yourself agreeing with my wife, there is a strong chance you do not have a soul.

It is now a little-known fact that TMP was the most expensive studio film made for its time. Of course, if mere expense were the benchmark of a great film, then *Pirates of the Caribbean 4: On Stranger Tides* would be ranked well above *Citizen Kane* by the AFI. However, in the case of *Star Trek: The Motion Picture*, the studio's vast expenditure of production resources led to the creation of a richly detailed science fiction universe; one that was already years in development, as TMP was upgraded to movie status during a time when Gene Roddenberry had already spent a significant amount of time and money developing its foundations for a spinoff of the original Star Trek television series for a proposed fourth television network under the Paramount aegis.

At a time when films like *Star Wars*, *Silent Running*, and *Alien* were busily moving the needle of science fiction production design toward a workmanlike, junkyardy aesthetic that presented the future (or the past, in the case of *Star Wars*) as shopworn and kludged together over generations, TMP presented an almost final gasp of the sleek, inherently optimistic, mid-century modern future foreseen in films like *2001: A Space Odyssey* and the seminal *Forbidden Planet*.

For better and worse, TMP is the most fully-realized, most epic version ever put on film of this starship-as-modern-hotel aesthetic. In this respect, TMP is unmatched even by the many Star Treks that would succeed it, since by the time the studio got around to making *Star Trek II: The Wrath of Khan*, newly-installed director Nicholas Meyer made the decision—for reasons both aesthetic, and due to budget cuts made as a response to the bloat of TMP—to revamp the Star Trek universe with a gritty nautical flair inspired by World War II submarine thrillers and the novels of C.S. Forester.

When Paramount Pictures greenlit TMP, the thinking behind the decision was extremely simple. George Lucas had just made enough money to purchase his own personal Endor with *Star Wars*: surely there was something in the studio's closet that could be quickly dusted off to not only compete, but also cash in on what studio heads must have then perceived as a fad with a limited window of opportunity. Today—when eighteen of the top twenty highest-grossing films of all time are science-fiction and fantasy (or some hybrid thereof)—it is hard to imagine a time when genre was so disreputable. In 1977, however, *Star Wars* was very much an outlier, and so, every effort had to be made to ensure that TMP was a "classy" production, a mainstream film with broad appeal beyond the Great Unwashed that once flooded NBC with letters for their beloved franchise's third-season renewal.

The choice of director Robert Wise, then, makes complete and perfect sense. A seasoned studio artisan and multiple Academy Award winner for classic films such as *West Side Story*, and *The Sound of Music*, Wise was also a genre adept whose films *The Day The Earth Stood Still*, *The Haunting*, and *The Andromeda Strain*, achieved popular success as well as good regard from the faithful. Oh yeah, and there's also the fact that he earned his first Oscar nomination for editing *Citizen* freakin' *Kane*.

In hindsight, however, the hiring of Wise feels a little tone deaf, considering that the goal was to drift off the success of *Star Wars*. While Wise was (and I'll fight anyone who says otherwise) a true artist of unimpeachable accomplishment—indeed, one of the finest directors ever produced by the Hollywood studio establishment—he was pretty much the antithesis of the young soul rebels who made Star Wars. Again, Lucas's methods may be the establishment now, but in the late 70's, his grainy, frenetically-edited, captured-in-documentary-style, and grittily-designed universe was part of the late stage of a revolutionary movement in independent, personal film making, and Robert Wise was as far from that vanguard as they got.

Of course, one might also argue that it was tone deaf to set up Star Trek as a competitor to *Star Wars* in the first place—especially in the marketplace of popular entertainment. Whereas *Star Wars* was a pulp-action fantasy space opera full of swashbuckling action and new-agey space wizards, *Star Trek* had always been more interested in intellectual concerns, moral dilemmas, and utopian futurism... with the occasional concession to military SF. While Paramount certainly got a glossy and respectable Big Budget Studio epic from Robert Wise, they sure as Surak didn't get *Star Wars*... and we're all the better for it.

Regardless of the reception TMP received in 1979 (initial commercial success eventually limited by critical disapproval), viewed outside of the commercial considerations of its time, the film serves as a fascinating bridge between Hollywood's classical era and the then-dawning age of the modern tentpole blockbuster. It is hard to imagine that there was a time when a franchise that still exists today was being directed by someone who worked on *Citizen Kane*!

Working in a widescreen format that was already falling out of fashion in mainstream film—but which was back then synonymous with Old School Hollywood Spectacles, like bible epics and war movies—Wise shows himself every bit the master of the mise-en-scene style of filmmaking. Like Orson Welles before him, Wise blocks his scenes in concert with the movement of the camera to create strong, pictorial frames in which cuts take place because they are motivated by the movement of the camera, which is in turn motivated by the movement of the actors, which is in turn motivated by the dramatic movement of the scene.

Where the dominant methodology in making today's films—especially major studio tentpole releases—is almost exclusively montage-driven (with the process involving the capture of as many angles on the action as possible, allowing filmmakers to then "find" the shape of the film and its individual scenes in the editing room) mise-en-scene work requires that a director make strong, defining choices about the final form of the material on the set. Montage-centered filmmaking allows greater flexibility after the fact to alter the pace, tone, and sometimes even the core story of a film, (something extremely useful in an environment in which films are test-screened and reshot multiple times in order to deliver to the audience the most satisfying experience possible). Mise-en-scene filmmaking generally requires a director to treat the script as final and plan accordingly—a dicey proposition in a film like TMP, which was rewritten so frequently through the course of its legendarily troubled production that script revisions arrived on the set not just with date stamps, but also hour stamps.

As a result, TMP may not always be the most gracefully written narrative, but, under Robert Wise's direction, it most certainly is a collection of elegantly choreographed picture frames depicting a wholly-designed artificial world. The camera moves when it has to, because it is motivated to do so by the action in the frame, and when it does, it is stately, like the Enterprise itself.

Working in this style, Wise forces himself to put all of his ingenuity toward the creation of painterly images with multiple levels of interest. Wise's frequent use of the split-diopter lens to create these frames is one of the most fascinating aspects of TMP as a master class in blocking and shooting scenes. The split-diopter allows multiple areas of the frame to stay in focus simultaneously, allowing for a tremendous amount of depth of field so that action can take place simultaneously over multiple planes without cutting away: the result often resembles and Old Master painting, with the deep focus capturing action and presenting story information on multiple levels from the extreme foreground to the far back.

By using this, and many other techniques—and choreographing his scenes with exquisite skill—Wise turns the Enterprise into a living, dynamic space without resorting to excessive camera movement or too accelerated an editing pattern: proving that "you are there" isn't merely a description that applies to the more modern, documentary-inspired style of directors like Paul Greengrass, or J.J. Abrams for that matter. While many fine directors have had their hand at putting the Star Trek Universe on film, few have done so with the artistic rigor and commitment shown by Robert Wise, and allowed by the TMP's massive budget and resources.

I say this because artistic rigor and commitment to an aesthetic are qualities that have become very fluid in today's digitally-enhanced, filmmaking: the flexibility (and cost savings) provided by shooting on digital media instead of costly film, as well as the infinite choices presented by non-linear editing has made the process of putting together a film malleable long past the release date. One of the hallmarks of montage-driven filmmaking is the overuse of close-up shots: both to punch up the emotional content of a scene, but also to cover up discrepancies in the position of the actors in the scenes because the flow and blocking of the scene has been altered in the editing. While Wise uses close-ups— what director doesn't?—he favors carefully positioned shots of multiple actors in various places in the frame when he cuts deeper into the scene from his master shot, selling the emotion of the moment not just by the intensity of the shot selection, but because the audience gets to watch the performers relate to—and build on—each other's work.

Because of Wise's directing style, the viewer of TMP gets to live in the Enterprise, and observe it and the characters and their relationships—both emotional and spatial—to one another in detail. While the film's admittedly slow pace may lead some viewers to wonder just HOW long they have to do this—to me, this style is something of a tonic in that it creates a mood and movement that feels organic to the type of story being told.

Like so much of the film's high-minded and idea-driven content, Wise's shooting style and scene design offers the space to appreciate not just the tale being told, and the sum of every artistic discipline that integrates into the greater whole of that story, but also the notion that this is a story about ideas, discovery, and the evolution of a soul... subjects which do not necessarily scream to be explored via hyperkinetic editing, a camera that moves as if wielded by a meth lemur, endless and massive close-up shots of actors, and scenes in which it is impossible to tell exactly where in the setting the characters began and ended.

So while Robert Wise may not have delivered a *Star Wars* competitor, he certainly delivered a Star Trek motion picture... and in delivering a Star Trek motion picture, Wise and his collaborators also delivered something that is redeemed from many of its considerable shortcomings by virtue of being magisterial, cinematic, thoughtful, and, again, occasionally, quite beautiful.

That much said, among all this beauty there are vast, heaping dollops of creamy yellow cheese... and there is one specific moment that encompasses all that is wincingly risible in Gene Roddenberry's hippy-dippy, utopian, up-with-people futurism—and his writing collaborators' ponderous groping toward rendering it as drama, and the huge amount of unintended homoerotic subtext, and the actors' often clumsy attempts to inhabit as middle-aged men roles they had not played in over a decade—and Robert Wise's attempts to wrap all of this in the bow of a major studio prestige release... all the while simultaneously embodying everything that is beautiful and worthwhile about Star Trek.

Recovering in sickbay after mind melding with "Vejur"—the massive and godlike creature of pure logic that is the film's main antagonist—Spock recognizes it to be barren of emotion. Finally realizing that his individual quest to rid himself of his own emotions in exchange for perfect logic is an evolutionary dead-end because it ignores the wisdom, and hope, that is gained from an appreciation of everything that is imperfect, Spock takes Kirk's hand and passionately declares, *"Jim, this simple feeling is beyond Vejur's comprehension."*

It can be difficult to love Star Trek as a fan. It has existed only slightly longer than I have, and as a result is a contemporary whose own maturation has been as rocky, embarrassing as that of any other adult: oftentimes moreso because it has always tried, and frequently failed, to appeal to whatever has been commercial in its time, and because it is not a creation that stems for a single source of monolithic ideas, but a colloquium of individuals—all trying to interpret Gene Roddenberry's vision for their own time. Star Trek can be many things, but as TMP shows us so well, often times those things include overwhelming amounts of "dated," and "cringeworthy."

You can call me an old fuddy-duddy for saying this—and, please know that I have tried my level best to keep this from being a "they don't make 'em like they used to" rant, because... well, a lot of the time they *really* shouldn't—but one of the things TMP has taught me over the years is that I like my Star Trek a little heady... and ponderous... and willing to walk the line between post-graduate smart and stoner-tedious by tackling science-fictional concerns like the emergence of a god-like consciousness that does not understand the value of the life with all of its flaws and foibles.

While Star Trek has never been a stranger to thrilling militaristic stories, and the sort of "us v. them" conflicts that are solvable with the application of force and sacrifice of lives, it has always attempted to wrap these, and all of its many stories around an interrogation of the inscrutability—and essential necessity—of that "simple human feeling" that Spock so poignantly discusses with his friend during the climax of TMP.

There are many reasons to show sympathy for The Motion Sickness. There are also an equal number of reasons to laugh at its excesses, incongruities, and fumbles... but Spock's epiphany is the grand summation that makes the entire enterprise worthwhile. *Star Trek: The Motion Picture* is a film of bad decisions—brought into the world by faulty logic, that somehow—through the combined talent of every artist tasked with its creation—overcomes that faulty logic by being a beautiful monument to the very value of faulty logic.

Defying every edict to entertain in the same way as the films with which it was supposed to compete, *Star Trek: The Motion Picture* instead takes its time, shows you a world, draws you into that world with a style that only seems old-fashioned, lets all of its inadequacies shine to the fullest of their capacity, and then uses all of those qualities to present a single idea that seems galactically silly at first... but somehow lingers in the mind in the years that follow, and ultimately unfolds into a human truth. It is a simple, yet infinitely complex reason to love a flawed film, and every time I watch it I find myself wondering how much better so many other films would be if they just made an effort to understand a concept so universal, yet fleeting, that even a character as wise, learned, and iconic as Mister Spock can only describe it as a "simple feeling."

Mrs. Yaga

MICHAL WOJCIK

AURELIA GREW UP IN A cabin a little ways outside of town, the one with the red mailbox and the twisted iron fence surmounted by skulls. Sometimes the house would groan and shift and flex its long chicken feet; every so often it would stretch out its legs, lifting Aurelia's room up over the trees and making crockery slide and smash. Then Mrs. Yaga would speak to the walls and soothe their domicile into settling back down again, to fold its legs like a hen does. An old black-and-white TV stayed perpetually switched on and soundless in the living room, drawing static off the aerial that spindled from the peak of the thatch roof. No wires came in off the main line but there was always power for the TV and the radio and the Mac Classic; as for a phone line, Mrs. Yaga had a cell.

"Did you have to do it, baba?" Aurelia asked as she washed dishes. She was nineteen , her hair black as electrical tape and her skin as white as bone. "He was so sweet."

"You think I took you under my roof just to let the next chłopak with a strong chin and a guitar sweep you away?"

Mrs. Yaga cackled, bending into a fridge that dated from the 40s at the very least. She didn't look like Aurelia's mother (because she wasn't), not even her grandmother (because she wasn't that either). She was *old*, gnarled like old branches left out in the sun and dry as a pomegranate husk, a collection of spikes and corners. She always wore fur over her shoulders, winter or summer. She always wore a necklace of claws from bears and wolves and tigers that clinked wherever she went.

"Greg doesn't play a guitar. He draws *webcomics*," Aurelia replied stubbornly, making the water splash with the vigour of her scrubbing.

Mrs. Yaga extracted an oversized egg coloured deep violet, clicking her tongue happily before slamming the fridge shut. One tap from her fingernail and a small hole cracked in the egg's top. She held that to her lips, slurping down its contents, liquid red and thick as blood dribbling down from the corners of her mouth. "Don't worry," she said. "If he's worthy of you he'll be back. The tasks are simple."

She wiped her chin clean with her sleeve and shook the shell, eliciting a dull rattle, then split it open on the counter. Out tumbled a foetus with a lizard's tail and a rooster's head, its eyes screwed shut tight. Mrs. Yaga held it up and squinted at it a moment before popping the creature into her mouth, crunching the bones with her pointed old teeth. She tossed the broken shell into the compost bin.

"All he has to do is bypass the gatekeeper of the thrice-tenth kingdom and bring me a fern flower, a dragon's heart, and a rusałka's lock of hair. Easy."

"They never come back," said Aurelia. "Not Daniel. Not Brendan. Not Steve." The three suitors never returned from their easy tasks: the first was killed by a great grizzly (unlike our grizzlies, the great grizzly is wise and terrible and prowls the Mountains of Dusk leaving the clean-picked corpses of mammoths in its wake); the second was frozen by a basilisk's stare; the third, less stupid than the others, simply wrote off Aurelia and her baba as irrational and ceased his romantic advances.

"You deserved better, my little chick. A girl with your hips needs a true bohater. Besides, I gave him a sword, which is more than I ever gave the others. Isn't that good enough?"

Aurelia bit back her next words, let the slosh of porcelain plates in water drift up over their absence. *Why must you do this to me? You aren't my mother. You aren't of my blood. I don't even know your first name; all the years I've been here you've only been baba to me.*

Mrs. Yaga leaned in closer, claws clicking together, unfelt wind stirring her wild white hair. She'd always seemed to know what Aurelia thought, her deep grey eyes filled with knowing. But now she only grunted before shuffling out of the kitchen, leaving Aurelia to wipe the counter and sweep the floor.

Mrs. Yaga had no steady job, received no regular income, or pension cheques. Whatever money she made came from the strange trinkets she sold every Thursday at the market: charms and amulets and love potions and little statues of Slavic gods that no Canadian would have known but that they bought anyway. Sometimes strangers would come from afar asking for private audience, promising countless rewards, but if Mrs. Yaga decided to aid them she seldom asked for cash. Instead she requested less tangible things: a stray dream caught in a web, a bundle of love letters exchanged before the First World War, their soft pencilled marks long faded into illegibility, the soul of a firstborn son. These she all kept in a great iron chest that doubled as a coffee table, until she had need of them.

As far as Aurelia knew she was one of these gifts, left here by her parents after some great favour, though Mrs. Yaga didn't keep her in the chest. Instead she ordered Aurelia about—to tend the cows and chickens and demons, keep the cabin clean, stoke the fire, cook meals, awaken the skulls at night so that their gazes would roam the yard like searchlights. In return, Mrs. Yaga taught her how to read and do arithmetic and advanced chemistry, how to speak Polish and Russian and Czech, how to churn butter and spin wool. Later, she tried to teach Aurelia how to chant spells, but Aurelia was rubbish at magic. She could sing the words prettily enough, but she could not make the words come true. She couldn't even transform a secret visitor into a pin to stick in her embroidery, to hide away from baba's prying—the most basic of spells for any ward of Mrs. Yaga.

The one thing Aurelia didn't learn much about was Mrs. Yaga herself. She was unaccountably old, and yet she seemed to have no past, no youth, as if she came into the world already bent and bruised. Only once had Mrs. Yaga relented to Aurelia's pestering about what her life had been before coming to Canada, saying, "I am a Yaga of a sisterhood of Yagas. When folk came across the water to this land from Ukraine and Poland and Russia, they brought their babas with them. I was a jędza baba of Poland, so I joined my sisters and crossed the sea in my mortar. Wherever the Slavs go, the Yagas follow."

That was as much an explanation as she ever gave.

Aurelia had a lingering sense that the old lady was always constantly appraising her with eyes that betrayed gnawing hunger. She feared that one day Mrs. Yaga would bake her in the oven and eat her, but that hadn't happened. Not yet, not for nineteen years.

The mortar still loomed in the attic, but these days Mrs. Yaga preferred driving the pickup she kept parked outside. The crone puttered into town that night, leaving Aurelia behind to lie in her room and listen to Greg's mix tape on her battered old Walkman and think on what life might've been like if she weren't Mrs. Yaga's ward, the people she might have met. The *boys* she might have met.

Since she turned thirteen, boys cast longing glances when she ran errands in town. They were terrified of Mrs. Yaga, though, who would grab tight hold of Aurelia with her bony fingers and affix any who stared with the evil eye. So when Aurelia started going out alone some years later, few men worked up the courage to talk to her. Even less to try and kiss her. And inevitably, if things went far enough and Aurelia couldn't keep the relationship a secret anymore (she never could keep secrets from Mrs. Yaga, baba knew them all) then her suitor would meet Mrs. Yaga and Mrs. Yaga would send him on a quest.

Poor Greg. He was by far her favourite. He'd come back from uni for the summer and would wait every week with a bouquet of hand-picked flowers on the path Aurelia took from the grocery store. She should have done more to resist his advances, drive him away, because now Mrs. Yaga had sent him to the thrice-tenth kingdom wherefrom few mortals could return.

The Walkman stopped playing, electromagnetic tape spilling out in one big tangle when Aurelia tried to pull the cassette free. She slipped off the headphones, threw the Walkman on the floor and balled her hands into fists. She grabbed a jacket and a shawl from the closet and then her handbag, and made her way up the twisty shambling staircase and the rickety ladder to the topmost floor.

She hesitated when she saw the mortar big and round and filled with shadow. She froze and listened for footsteps or the sound of a truck pulling into the driveway. All she heard were the usual pops and groans and whispers of the house. A thrill shook her, fear and excitement tangling as she gripped the long pestle leaning against the wall beside the skis and bicycle wheels, and the pestle seemed to respond, warming to her touch. Aurelia took it with her to the shutters and threw them open, startling the ravens perched on the ledge beyond. Dust swirled up in the wind, motes catching the dying sunlight before blowing away.

She leaned on the pestle and looked out over the road and the forest for one long moment before squaring her shoulders and turning back, hoisting herself into the pestle's bowl. The inside was dark and moist against her legs and thighs. It too responded to her, accepting her, letting her settle in its maw, and when she pushed against the floorboards with the pestle, the mortar rose a few inches into the air then lurched in an unsteady spinning way towards the open window.

Aurelia fought the wobble that threatened to spill her, brought the pestle around like a paddle and hastily rowed at the sky. She'd never ridden the mortar before, but she'd seen Mrs. Yaga depart in its embrace and she'd read the old books in the library, the ones written in Old Church Slavonic by hand on vellum, and she'd also gone canoeing once or twice. So she succeeded in steadying the beastly container as she passed the window frame and out over the yard. Her brow furrowed in determination as she swiftly brought the mortar to bear, passing beyond the fence, beyond this sleepy town in northern British Columbia, and over the wavering boundary to the thrice-tenth kingdom.

An hour elapsed before Aurelia spotted the lair of the dragon under starlight and moonlight, the entrance to its cavern folded between the heels of the Mountains of Dusk. Smoke billowed from there in intertwining streams, threading together like rope. *I'll wait for him here*, Aurelia thought, directing the mortar to descend onto the narrow path to the dragon's gates. She stowed the pestle away and hoisted herself out from the bowl, her legs cramped and muscles aching, and she tumbled indelicately in the dirt. When she lifted her head, she saw something glimmer in the rocks above her, and she reached into her handbag for a flashlight before wandering up the path.

It was the sword. A sabre, its hilt hammered together in the form of an eagle's head. The flashlight's beam went this way and that, lancing the sheer cliffs above before settling on Greg's footprints leading down from the mountain. Then it moved to a great disturbance of shattered boulders, tumbled stone. Gregory had seen the dragon, that was plain. He'd dropped the sword and fled.

Aurelia took up the blade and sat on a nearby stone, idly contemplating the size, the weight, before her gaze went back to the dragon's cave and the smoke that issued in puffs with each of the dragon's breaths. Then back down the path, to wherever Greg might be. He was probably back in British Columbia, the thrice-tenth kingdom peeling away until he emerged on some highway somewhere and hitched a ride back home. Memories of rusałki and other forest demons would fade until they became but dreams, mere fodder for essays while he completed his folklore degree. He would forget Aurelia, too, and all she'd have left of Greg would be wilted flowers and a broken mix tape.

Why do they always listen to Mrs. Yaga? Are they so afraid, that they'd rather chance the thrice-tenth kingdom than whisk me away themselves? Do they think I'm someone they can own, something they can barter for? Aren't I prize enough without a quest attached?

And lastly: *A fucking **mix tape**?*

*No. **Fuck** no. A man needed to do more than that. **I** need to do more than that.*

Aurelia gripped the sabre tight and headed up the path towards the smell of ash and brimstone.

Mrs. Yaga was waiting in the yard by the chicken coup when Aurelia glided down in the mortar. Three months had gone by, three long hard months etched into Aurelia's face and the cracked skin of her hands. Her jeans and jacket were replaced by a Polish peasant's dress and cloak of deepest indigo. The old witch said nothing when Aurelia clambered out from the pestle and reached in again for a rough leather sack. The young woman said nothing when she opened the mouth and deposited the sack's contents at Mrs. Yaga's feet.

A delicate flower with five golden petals each the size of a hand, a ghostly white light at its centre flicking about like a cat's pupil. It smelled of mangos. A bound cord of sea-green hair. A heart that glowed with inner fire, not much larger than a human heart, and yet clearly the heart of something other.

Mrs. Yaga stared into Aurelia's eyes and a smile touched those cracked and bloody lips. "Why did you bring these to me? You are no suitor, my little chick. I did not send you on this quest."

They stared at each other a while longer, measuring.

"I am my own suitor," answered Aurelia.

"Ah." Mrs. Yaga nodded, then she thrust her chin towards the mortar. "You stole that from me."

"You weren't using it."

Mrs. Yaga clicked her tongue, stooped and dug her fingers into the dragon's heart, hefting it, admiring the glow.

"I—" Aurelia began, stopped herself, began again. "I always wondered, why only the men were allowed to be bohaterowie. Why you only gave quests to them."

Mrs. Yaga shook her head. "I never gave quests to *them*. The fools would never have finished them, never would have trodden the dark paths of the world's mirror and emerged unscathed. It was not in their hearts." She paused, pierced Aurelia with her gaze. "The quests were for *you*, when you realized you had strength to complete them. Your training is done, Aurelia Wiśniewska. You may go where you will."

Aurelia swallowed, nodded. "Thank you, baba."

"Don't mention it." Mrs. Yaga was already shuffling towards the cabin, waving a hand dismissively, and Aurelia watched as the mortar slowly wobbled after its master.

Then she turned to the gate, and the road, and the world beyond the fence of skulls, and began to walk.

The End

Is Fantasy Writing Gendered?

KATE ELLIOTT

SOME TIME AGO I WAS asked this common question:

Do you think there's a difference in the way males and females write fantasy?

In essentials? No.

I'm defining art in its broadest sense here: art as image, words, music, shape, movement, textiles, design, and so on, works that come out of the human mind, heart, and hands interacting with whatever intangible spirit sparks us to create and experiment.

Art is so deeply wired into the human psyche that I think art is inextricable from humanness. All humans have the capacity for art, for curiosity, for exploration and creation.

Art is not our biology or our gender.

However, cultures define what counts as art, and therefore who has historically been allowed to create art or be labeled as an artist has often been related to biology or gender as seen through the lens of an individual's culture.

So: Do I think there are differences in the way males and females write fantasy?

I think there are differences in the way individuals write fantasy, and then in our culture those differences tend to get mapped onto a gender axis because our culture is comfortable defining and patterning things along the gender axis as if differences between genders are more important than differences between individuals.

Bear in mind that I am speaking in this context (of difference) about behavior, temperament, personality, and how the creative drive manifests. The creative drive doesn't manifest in the uterus or the penis (nor need we lock definitions of gender into those organs).

However, it might be possible to quantify some weighted differences between men and women writing fantasy in USA/UK commercially marketed fantasy today.

As far as I know, no one has done a study of the last 30 or 40 years of the science fiction and fantasy fields in which they analyze something as simple as character presence in fantasy fiction. The closest I've found is an article by writer Nicola Griffith with an analysis of 15 years worth of award-winning fiction: "The more prestigious the award, the more likely the subject of the narrative will be male."[1]

Do male writers mostly write about male protagonists? How about female writers? What about the percentages of secondary characters? Do male writers disproportionately populate their worlds with male characters (including protagonists and minor characters) overall, in a way not consistent with the actual presence of people in the world? That is, rather than showing a world in which there is an approximate 50/50 split of male to female characters, do these worlds foreground and give speaking roles to far more male characters than female? And if female characters are represented, are they represented in only a few limited types of roles, and how does the writer allow them to function both within the society and within the story?

What about female writers? Do they tend to have more female characters throughout their books? In a wider variety of roles, with more agency and importance? Or do they often rep-

1 https://nicolagriffith.com/2015/05/26/
books-about-women-tend-not-to-win-awards/

licate the same demographics as male writers?

What about queer writers? As more people in US & UK culture challenge the idea of innate binary gender roles that shift, too, will influence how fantasy is written in and for any specific market.

My feeling is that the idea that males and females "write fantasy differently" has more to do with emphasis. Because in addition to the quantifiable issue of character presence, there is also the issue of what actions, events, details, and experiences are emphasized, *or perceived to be emphasized,* in any given story.

I personally don't believe these vectors of emphasis have much to do with biologically quantifiable essentialist differences of mind and creativity. Even if there were some (and it would be very difficult to quantify differences in creativity), it would be practically impossible to tease out what those were from the morass of cultural expectations and assump-tions through which we slog on a day to day basis.

Emphasis and "worthiness" can be culturally influenced by unexamined assumptions about what matters enough to be written about or noticed. So in that sense it's a little difficult to say that men write differently than women BECAUSE of their gender rather than because of what culture tells us about gender. It's a subtle difference, but if we're talking about "real" potential differences in writing, this is a crucial one.

I think we carry exceedingly strong cultural expectations about gender and about the past, and especially about ideas about "how" the past "was" that often ignore or deem unimportant entire swathes of human existence. I think we still often assume that a male point of view combined with the heterosexual male gaze (seeing things from a particular set of assumptions about what is important and worthy) is the norm. So it is perfectly possible to pick up an epic fantasy novel in which almost all the characters are male, and women practically invisible, and somehow think there is nothing exceptional or even wrong about a depiction of a world in which women barely exist. To me these are flawed depictions and bad world building. They're not "male" or "female."

If I want to write two women talking to each other about something other than a man (see also The Bechdel/Wallace Test for films), does that make my writing "girly?" If a man does it, does that make his writing "girly?" Are male writers more likely to have only one or a handful of female characters, few of whom ever talk to each other or relate in a meaningful way? Are female writers more likely to emphasize female relationships within a story? If so (and I don't have the stats to back up either of those assertions), I would call these choices cultural and experiential, not biological.

Anyway, what is "male" and "female?" To what degree are our ideas about how things are gendered writing in fact specific to the culture we grew up in or are writing about?

If I want to write about clothes or sewing, then am I "writing female" even though tailoring was and is a male occupation in many societies? What if the character who discusses clothes is a male tailor whose livelihood relies on his knowledge and expertise? Would it be more "male" if he only talked about the tools he used, like his sewing machine or his sharps and blunts, rather than fabric and design?

How about the perception that women write extraneous romance into their books because that is a feminine thing to do, while love stories in male-written books are glossed-over as a narratively-appropriate part of the story?

Let me give two more examples.

I'm an athlete; from toddlerhood I've always had an active, fitness and outdoors-oriented personality. That often gives me more in common with other people, regardless of gender, who have a similar "athletic" orientation than with "All Women Everywhere," many of whom I may happen to have little in common with both by temperament and interests (as well as experience and background). At the same time, I grew up in a time when "playing sports" was deemed an ineluctably masculine endeavor (even though some women have always found ways to be active and play sports). A relative once remarked that his young son was "all boy" because of the son's budding interest in playing sports; this despite me (rather than the relative) being the one who played sports all through secondary school.

So if I have written several athletic and active heroines and heroes, does that make my writing masculine? Are my athletic heroines commented on differently from my athletic heroes? Is athleticism deemed a normal part of male-ness such that active male heroes don't need commenting on at all while (despite all evidence to the contrary) some people continue to remark on women being active, adventurous, and athletic as if that trait and interest is unfeminine? Why should a propensity toward being active and athletic be a gendered trait AT ALL when we clearly see it expressed in all manner of people (of various genders), meanwhile other people (of various genders) aren't drawn to athletic pursuits?

Meanwhile, I don't really enjoy shopping (except for books and in office supply stores) while my spouse (a former police officer <== see what I did there?) loves nothing more than exploring antique stores, junk shops, and swap meets. If he were to write a story in which a male anthropologist detective hero spends time contentedly browsing in an antique store and ends up finding a peculiar item that later becomes important to the plot, would that make his writing feminine? If a male writer describes every gun or sword with loving precision while a female writer describes dresses in similar close focus, is that a gendered difference (guns v gowns)? What if she lovingly describes knives while he minutely describes food and feasts? Does the desire to describe objects in detail and make that description part of the story mean these two writers have more in common with each other as writers than, say, with writers who eschew description and focus on action?

What if, by focusing on a narrow, particularist vector of analysis, we ignore the ways in which writers of different genders have similarities that may make them more alike than different?

Until we have actual data on such questions rather than anecdotal information or suppositions based on "what everyone knows" or on our assumptions about how things must be based on the last two books we read, I think we can't draw any firm conclusions about gender differences in writing sff.

A Closed and Common Orbit

ANA GRILO

OPTIMISTIC, FEEL-GOOD, ADVENTUROUS AND FUN: *A Closed and Common Orbit*, Becky Chambers' standalone follow-up to *The Long Way to a Small, Angry Planet* is as good, smart and satisfying as its predecessor.

There is a great success story behind these novels too. *The Long Way to a Small, Angry Planet* started as a self-published book and when word of mouth and excellent reviews started to spread, the book was picked up by UK publisher Hodder & Stoughton. It's probably safe to say that that first novel became a 2015 *sensation* collecting award nominations like it was running out of time, among them the prestigious Arthur C. Clarke Award. It was also longlisted for the Baileys Women's Prize for Fiction as well as the Tiptree Award.

I like to think that its success story is indicative of a new direction within SFF: more optimistic, feel good, humane stories that celebrate ordinary people against an extraordinary, futuristic backdrop.

What's so great about this? The optimism of this series does not solely rely on its characters succeeding or simple being/doing good. Its optimism equally appear in the way that very foundation of this universe is composed of a diverse make-up that is almost intoxicating in its normalisation. Take for instance this short, unremarked sentence right at the beginning of *A Closed and Common Orbit* when one of the main characters, an AI who has a new human body, looks at her new "kit" and describes it (bold mine):

"The kit looked like it had been pulled straight from the "Human" example in an interspecies relations textbook: **brown skin, black hair, brown eyes**. She was thankful that the kit's manufacturer had seen the wisdom of **blending in**."

There is no fuss about it: this is simply who humans *are*.

A genetically modified engineer and an artificial intelligence walk into a bar...

A Closed and Common Orbit picks up right after the final events of *The Long Way to a Small, Angry Planet*, with the once-Lovelace Artificial Intelligence, now reset and memory-less, finding a new life aboard a new body. Before, Lovelace had eyes everywhere and her task was to care for the health and well-being of the Wayfarer's crew. Now, renamed Sidra, she finds herself in a new–and illegal–synthetic body, trying to cope with a limited, isolated, and physical existence that simply doesn't seem *enough*.

She is helped by Pepper, an engineer who risked everything to get Sidra up and running. Pepper is a genetically modified clone, previously one of the Janes–Jane23–and part of a slave class of junk-fixers, brought up within a factory without any knowledge that there was an outside world. When Jane was ten years old, an accident at the factory led to a scape–and a new life inside a ship found in a junkyard. The ship's AI Owl becomes Jane's family.

With chapters alternating between Sidra/now and Jane/before, we follow both characters (as well as Owl, arguably a main character in this space drama too) as they journey through their lives. It's a story about adapting, surviving, changing–identity is the core and just like its predecessor, *A Closed and Common Orbit* also has many things to say about found families, friendship and love. It also features different alien species, elegant gender fluidity, and a superb plotline that starts with loss and change and ends up with a quest and a *heist*. "Cool" does not even begin to describe it.

Imagine: one person whose life was so limited she didn't even KNOW that there was such a thing as a "sky" or "edible food" (when you consumed liquid food all your life, do you even know how to chew?). Another one whose life was lived inside the confines of a ship and in downloading to a body and given the universe, THAT'S when the limitation starts: for an AI, a universe is not enough, if you don't have connectivity. The questions of what connectivity even is, and what makes a person human fill the story to the brim. The answers are never straight-forward and following these lovable, interesting characters confronting and interrogating those questions is only a small part of the joy in reading this novel.

If there was such a thing as a Cosy Space Opera subgenre of Speculative Fiction, Becky Chambers' series would likely be listed alongside the equally excellent *On a Red Station, Drifting* by Aliette de Bodard and *Binti* by Nnedi Okorafor.

Rating: 8 out of 10.

Writing the Strange Side of Japan

JIM ZUB

PEOPLE SAY YOU SHOULD "WRITE what you know."

They're not wrong, but I think it's also important to stretch yourself beyond your own personal experiences. Learning about somewhere else and expanding your worldview is a great way to open yourself up to new stories. These are all things I've learned while writing a series called *Wayward*, published by Image Comics.

The quick sales pitch for *Wayward* is "It's like *Buffy* in Japan" and that tagline works wonders at conventions when I'm trying to explain it to a potential customer in 10 seconds or less to pique their interest. It's not a perfect fit, but as pitches go it's pretty good. The series is about teenagers battling traditional Japanese monsters on the streets of modern Tokyo, with bigger ideas about mythology, generational divide, and coming of age thrown in for good measure.

I started working on *Wayward* because an artist named Steven Cummings, who lives in Yokohama and is raising a family there, wanted to work with me on a story. When we started jamming ideas we came back to a concept he had about telling supernatural stories in Tokyo. The real Tokyo, not the one you see in movies or cartoons where it's only high-rise buildings or ninja temples. Steven wanted to show the actual city full of incredible variety, robust history, and distinctive neighborhoods, each one a fascinating hub of business, social hierarchy, and tradition. Steven loves Tokyo and wanted readers to see the depth and breadth the city had to offer. I foolishly offered to write stories so we could do just that.

What I quickly realized is I'd thrown myself into the deep end on writing places and people from a very different background from myself. I'd traveled to Japan for business several times and had a deep love of the people and places, but this wasn't just a tourist-worthy glance, it was meant to be something far more in-depth. Steven and I were going to weave traditional Yokai (Japanese mythological spirits and creatures) into a modern setting and use the real city as the foundation for those stories and real culture as the inspiration for our characters.

I started with expanding my understanding of Yokai stories. Like fables and fairy tales from Europe or other countries, Yokai stories grew out of a need to codify behaviours and fictionalize lessons about life, love, and well-being. They're stories about intense emotions, moral failings, or the unexplained. Just like stories about dragons or vampires, tales of the Yokai have been told and retold hundreds of times - adapted, twisted, changed. We realised we had room to respectfully make our own mark on them without feeling like we were betraying the source material.

Beyond those supernatural elements though, I had to stop making assumptions and start really digging into to research. Research about culture, traditions, history, folklore, and language. Extensive discussion about where I thought the story could go and how that would be impacted by setting it in modern Japan.

At first I felt really limited and slammed up against a bunch of unexpected roadblocks. I kept bouncing plot ideas off Steven and he'd carefully explain that they wouldn't happen that way, not in Tokyo. A student couldn't skip classes without their parents being immediately notified. A ruined building wouldn't be left unattended for long periods of time. Police procedure and "due process" as we know it in North America isn't the same. Each idea I'd brainstorm had to go through a cultural filter and every time I got it "wrong" it intimidated the heck out of me.

Thankfully, more research and discussion started to point the way. Instead of looking at the differences as limitations, I tried to understand what they meant and how we could incorporate them into the story.

Ohara Emi, a very traditional teenage girl in *Wayward* and the viewpoint character of the book's second arc grew out of what I learned about the family unit in Japan. Her struggles to define herself as an individual and live her own life while trying to please her family reflect larger cultural issues Japan is going through as it tries to hold onto tradition while simultaneously embracing more modern influences. It's a glimpse into a microcosm of Japan and a way for us to understand that struggle on a micro and macro level.

Getting into Ohara's mindset was tough (and it still is) but telling her story gives us a point of view many North American readers haven't seen before. She doesn't make the decisions we would make at her age, and often reflect a more traditionally Japanese approach to conflict. I wanted to build up reader empathy with her, even when she's not doing what the reader expects, as a touchstone for getting to know a bit more about one of the many aspects of Japanese culture. I think that, in and of itself, has value.

It's not all about the differences though. There are universal experiences that act as a bridge to our North American readers. The fear of entering adulthood or finding yourself somewhere brand new and not knowing where you belong, those are situations we've all lived through. They're emotional anchor points we use to build our story and, when done well, they ring true to all of us.

Writing about Japan is both frustrating and rewarding. It takes three to four times longer for me to write a *Wayward* script compared to any other comic script writing I do, because each part gets worked and re-worked to fit the culture and the places in the story. The storytelling shortcuts I've built up over the years on other stories rarely work in *Wayward* and it forces all of us on the team to work harder to get it right. We're far from perfect but, when I hear from Japanese readers or expats who lived in Japan that *Wayward* feels authentic in its portrayal of Tokyo, it makes the time and effort feel worthwhile.

Working on *Wayward* has taught me a lot about collaboration, research, and the potential that comes from delving deeper for a story. It's also taught me you can write about another culture respectfully while bringing something new into the mix.

People say you should "write what you know."

They're not wrong, but you can push yourself to know a lot and broaden your horizons at the same time. Dig in, do the research and connect yourself to something new. Storytelling is about building empathy. Empathy for characters, places, or a particular point of view. It's about creating a bond between the creator and the audience. In order to do that effectively you have to be able to see past yourself and see other people, other environments, and attitudes beyond your own.

Ruby

ANNA HIGHT

"HEY, BABY," HE SAID. "WHAT is *up*?"

The man stood on the stoop, dragging from a joint (she could smell the smoke off of it, dank and heady and just this side of sweet), but as soon as Ruby passed him by he pulled the joint away from his mouth and spat on the ground. It landed near her left foot with a nauseating slap.

Ruby lifted her chin, stared straight ahead and kept walking.

"C'mon, baby," he said. His voice seeped from between his lips, thick and warm and blood-like. Ruby's mouth watered. Her stomach rolled. "Don't be rude."

Don't be rude. Her mother liked to say that to her, too. *You so mean, girl. Somebody pays you a compliment, you just take it. Why you got to be so mean to people, you just like Abuela, thinkin' everybody out to get you. They don't mean nothing by it. It's just them being nice.*

It didn't *feel* nice, though. Not to Ruby. Their "compliments" stuck to her skin and weighed her down, like dirty, humid city air, the kind that made it hard to breathe. From the corner of her eye Ruby caught his gaze drifting down over her bare legs. She felt his eyes lingering at the hem of the red skirt that ended just above her knees. It felt like something hot and viscous, stuck to her skin.

"Nice legs," he said.

It was her favorite, that red skirt, and of course her mother had warned her about wearing it. *You shouldn't,* she'd said, *It's too short. You'll get cold.*

Except that it was late September and an oppressive heat still hung over the city, the hot, dying breath of Indian summer. Through every sidewalk grate that she crossed, a blast of warm, putrid air erupted from the subway below, lifting her skirt ever so slightly, revealing an extra inch of thigh.

You just asking for trouble, Ruby's mother had said, when she'd come downstairs wearing the skirt despite her mother's protests. *It's your own fault if anything happens.*

That was true. It *would* be her fault, if anything happened. Ruby never argued with that.

She reached the corner and stopped to wait for the red light. The man on the stoop pinched out and pocketed his joint and tripped down the steps to sidle up next to her, peering at her face with a crooked smile. "You ain't bein' very nice," he said. "What's the matter, you shy?"

She wasn't shy, not at all, but she knew that men preferred her that way. They didn't like it when she met their gazes, didn't like it when she talked back. They needed her to be quiet, meek, shy. She didn't like to think too long about why.

Ruby stared down at her feet, lips pressed together.

"Fuckin' cunt," said the man, when she didn't answer. The light changed and Ruby quickly started across the street. The man followed a few paces behind. Every footstep made her throat close up, her heart race, her mouth water more, though she couldn't tell if it was because she was going to be sick or because she was hungry. She couldn't remember the last time she'd eaten.

"Slut," he said.

He tailed her for half a block, alternating between spitting on the sidewalk and calling her names under his breath. They weren't anything new, nothing she hadn't heard before. Different men, different days, always the same shit.

People passed them by. Ruby could tell they heard what he was saying, could see the look on her face. They ducked their heads as they walked on a little faster. Said nothing. No one interfered.

Eventually, the man managed to dart in front of her, forcing her to stop and look up at him. "Where you goin' in such a hurry?" he asked. Ruby could see little flecks of spit at the corners of his mouth.

"My abuela's," she said. Her mother would have a lot to say about her talking to strangers. *Don't you go lookin' for trouble, girl. God, you always lookin' for trouble.* "She's sick."

"That's too bad," said the man. He held out a hand. "You should come home with *me*."

She side-stepped around him and resumed walking. It was getting dark. *Ain't good for a girl to be out after the sun goes down*, her mother'd said. *Bad stuff happens. Don't you be one of them girls. Anything happen, it'll be your own fault.*

Ruby *was* one of those girls.

No sense denying it, her grandmother had once said, while picking something out of her teeth.

The bodega on the corner had a sign that advertised pomegranates for sale, $2.49 each. Ruby loved pomegranates. She loved to cut and break them open, dig out the slippery insides and suck the flesh off the seeds until they were bare. She loved the mess they made, though her mother did not. *Can't you eat like a normal person*, she would say. *Just like Abuela, you got no manners. Why can't you act right?*

Ruby loved that pomegranates were red, like her skirt, like her name.

"Come on." The man grabbed for her arm but she dodged him easily. She saw an alley, just two blocks from her grandmother's building. She'd mentioned it once, had told her that hardly anyone ever used it. "A good place," she had warned, "to get trapped."

Ruby darted toward it.

"Where you going?" called out the man, jogging a little to keep up with her, to chase her down the block. People walked past, and still no one said anything.

"Don't," she warned. Ruby looked back and held out her hands, palms out. They were shaking slightly, she couldn't really help it, not with the adrenaline rushing through her, thrumming through her like an electric current. "Please."

"Shit." The man laughed at her, a big laugh that showed his fat tongue, his dirty teeth. Ruby's mouth watered more. Her stomach twisted and turned. "You playin' games with me, little girl?"

The alley was empty except for dumpsters and trash cans, the windows too high to reach without climbing up and into the fire escapes. It ended with a sagging, chain-link fence that separated it from an empty lot. Ruby turned back and faced the man, her legs slightly apart, boots planted firmly on the pavement.

"Come on, mami," said the man, a sideways smile on his thin-lipped mouth. The color of it reminded Ruby of spoiled meat. "I'm gonna make you feel real good."

He approached her. She let him. Her mother's voice rattled around in her head. *Always lookin' for trouble.* She could hear televisions blaring over her head, the sound of cars on the streets, a siren howling in the distance, the bark of a dog somewhere nearby. She glanced up at the darkening sky, a fat moon slowly rising over the tops of the building.

"Leave me alone," she whispered, the words summoned deep from her throat. A warning.

"C'mon," said the man, reaching out to touch her arm. She shivered. "You wanna party, baby girl?"

"Yes," Ruby said. She bared her teeth, small but sharp and gleaming white in the moonlight. "Let's party."

She went for his throat so he couldn't scream.

It was all red, like a pomegranate.

"How was the walk?" asked her grandmother, croaking the last word into the Kleenex she held to her mouth. Ruby helped her sit down in the chair by the door and dropped the bag from the fruit stand on the kitchen table.

"This is from everybody," said Ruby, handing her grand-mother an envelope. The card was signed by the whole family; the little kids had scrawled their names all over the front and the back, in festive Crayola greens and blues.

There was a tiny, tell-tale red smear on one corner of the envelope. Ruby's own sort of signature. Her grandmother touched it and inspected the flecks it left behind on the pad of her thumb. She tsked softly.

"Did something happen?" she asked. She opened her card and smiled at the cheerful bear on the outside, read the sappy yet sincere note inside. She got up with effort and stuck it to the fridge with a magnet that said #1 Grandma.

"Sí," said Ruby. She got out a bowl and passed one of the pomegranates to her grandmother. "And it was all my fault."

"It always is." Her grandmother dug sharp nails into the sides of the pomegranate and easily cracked it apart, send-ing its seeds cascading into the bowl. She picked one up with sticky fingers and popped it into her mouth.

The grin she gave Ruby was almost wolfish.

Where to Start With Portal Fantasies

SEANAN MCGUIRE

THE TERM "PORTAL FANTASY" IS often treated as synonymous with "children's story." A child, eager for adventure or needing to learn a lesson—or both—falls through a doorway or portal of some kind and finds themselves in a strange new world, one which happens to have been perfectly designed to teach them what they need to know before packing them up and sending them home, older, wiser, and finally ready to take up their rightful place as productive members of society. The best cure for wanting magical adventures, in a portal fantasy world, is actually *having* a magical adventure.

This is meant to be a sort of "starter kit" essay, telling you where to begin with the portal fantasy genre, but the odds are good, if you've grown up reading English-language science fiction and fantasy, that you've encountered the portal fantasy already. Baum's Oz, Carroll's Wonderland, Barrie's Neverland, and Lewis's Narnia are all "classic" portal fantasies, texts which have managed, rightly or wrongly, to become definitional for the genre. In all four, a child or children from our world is carried to a fantastic new place through some force of nature (a twister, gravity) or magical device (Peter Pan, a strange wardrobe), and adventure ensues.

Interestingly, although many definitions of the portal fantasy will involve going once and never again, in three of these four, the child or children, having once traveled, will travel again. Dorothy even winds up choosing Oz on a permanent basis, and there is an air to the Alice stories which implies that she might have done the same if she'd been allowed. Only Wendy and Susan are eventually denied the sanctuary of their magical worlds, and in both cases, for the same reason: they grew up. Being an adult—especially being an adult woman—is often treated as an impassable barrier in the portal fantasy, the one monster that can't be defeated with a vorpal blade or a bucket of water.

My first portal fantasies were found in cartoons. Television in the 1980s had seized on the idea that there could be a magical world just behind the nearest door or over the nearest rainbow, and splashed it liberally across Saturday mornings. *My Little Pony and Friends, Dungeons and Dragons, The Fluppy Dogs,* and even *The Care Bears* were all classic portal fantasies, with normal children falling into magic and being forced to fight their way home—assuming they wanted to return at all. Children taken by the Care Bears would normally have one adventure, maybe two, before going back to their normal lives. Megan and her siblings, upon being taken to Ponyland, never went back. Sometimes the happy ending in a portal fantasy is running away forever.

But this is, again, a primer. I'll assume, for the sake of argument, that you've encountered some or all of the classics, and that, if not, the authors and settings listed above will tell you where to start. That's a lot of required reading for a relatively small sub-genre, true, but those particular stories form the cultural underpinnings of so much modern genre fiction that it's worth it.

So what has portal fantasy done for us lately?

If you reach the end of your required reading angry on behalf of Susan and Wendy and all the other girls who found the doors to magic slammed in their faces as soon as they grew up, Barbara Hambly's got your back, with her Windrose Chronicles, beginning with *The Silent Tower* and continuing into *The Silicon Mage*. The first of these came out in 1986, so the tech is fairly dated but internally consistent, and seeing an adult woman—a nerd, even—having a magical adventure was so important to me when I stumbled across them. It's an epic adventure, an epic love story, and a beautiful adult portal fantasy.

Or maybe you're looking for more portal fantasies aimed at the children we were and the children we love to share stories with, Catherynne Valente's *The Girl Who Circumnavigated Fairyland in a Ship of Her Own Making* is a classic portal fantasy, by turns whimsical and brutal, utterly suitable for reading either as a solo adult or as someone looking for a story they can read with their kids. The series is finished now, which means it has a solid conclusion and won't make you wait. Lucky you!

Or maybe you're aching from the contradictions between our world and the worlds on the other side of the portal, yearning for explanation, for resolution, for something to make it all make sense. In that case, I heartily recommend Sarah Rees Brennan's *The Turn of the Story*, which tidily sets many of the classic portal fantasy tropes on their ears, sending the irascible Elliot over the wall and into a story he's not entirely sure he knows how to deal with.

These three worlds—Ferryth, Fairyland, and the Border—couldn't be more different, but between them, they'll ground you in what modern portal fantasy has to offer. There are so many others, from authors ranging from Stephen King to Diana Wynne Jones, and the adventure is only just beginning. That's the best thing about adventure. It's always only just beginning, even when you're in the middle of it all.

All you need to do is open a door.

The Scourge

THEA JAMES

IN THE LAND OF KELDAN, one thing is certain: you do not want to be afflicted with the Scourge. The disease first appeared three hundred years ago, ripping through the country and killing a third of the population. Now, centuries later, Keldan still wrestles with the scars of that disease—the people of the river country were accused of originating the virus, and have been ostracized from the "civilized" population of townsfolk in the valley below. The powerful leader of Keldan, Governor Felling and her reign of exploitation and greed hasn't helped matters, and the divide between river people "grubs" and townspeople "pinchworms" continues to grow (just as the divide continues to grow between Keldan and its neighboring kingdoms).

And then, the worst thing finally happens: The Scourge returns.

Sweeping through the prisons, and then slowly making its way to the general Keldan population, the Scourge kills without discrimination—the telltale fever, rash, and excruciating pain are quick to strike and impossible to cure.

In order to save her people, Governor Felling decides to institute a quarantine for all of those exhibiting early symptoms. Attic island, off the coast of Keldan, has become a colony for the ill, where the Scourge victims are put to hard labor and to live or die. Of course, no one who has ever been sent to Attic Island ever returns.

Enter Ani, a headstrong young woman and child of the river people, who happens to be in the wrong place at the wrong time. When she and her best friend Weevil are captured by the Wardens who scour the woods for potential Scourge sufferers, Ani is desperate to save her friend, and to escape from certain death. Accompanied by a young town girl—a spoiled pinchworm named Della, who seems determined to despise Ani at first sight—the outlook for Ani and Weevil seems desperate. But if these three can work together, and uncover the true nature of the Scourge and their new prison home, they might be able to save everyone and everything they love from certain death.

I've been a big fan of Jennifer A. Nielsen's ever since reading *The False Prince*—one of my favorite fantasy novels (and top 10 overall novels) of 2012, the year of its release. Many of the things I loved so much about that book are present here, in *The Scourge.*

The biggest draw of this standalone fantasy novel—besides the fact that it's a lovely, true standalone novel—is the characters. Narrated from Ani's first person point of view, *The Scourge* immediately sets a funny, direct, and simple tone that is, frankly, refreshing to read in the YA/upper-MG fantasy space. One thing I love so much about Ani is that her voice never feels forced or inauthentic—very similar to Sage, the wise-cracking, upbeat protagonist of *The False Prince*. Ani is forthright, for the most part, and while she has her own smart-talking and wise-cracking tendencies, she's also hilariously wonderful in her reasoning process—e.g. sure, she won't steal medicine right away, she'll just wait until the time is right for her to sneak a sip or two, later.

The most impressive thing about The Scourge, though, lies with the three main characters and the ribbon of friendship that runs throughout the novel. There's a particularly painful scene between Weevil and Ani, as both of them try their hardest to save the other from brutal punishment at the hands of a Warden; there's also the entire growth arc for the relationship between Ani and her nemesis (or is she), Della.

On the negative front, however, The Scourge leaves a few things to be desired on the plotting and world-building fronts. While I love a good standalone fantasy novel—especially in the middle grade and young adult spaces—The Scourge is an example of an area where I wish there was *more* to the world and the backstory. Everything in this novel felt didactic and heavy-handed. Similarly, the twists regarding the disease, the villainy of certain characters, all of this was incredibly easy to predict and see from the outset of the book. Unlike, say, The False Prince, which may have been easy to guess, but executed its twists with a deftness and

humor that's missing in *The Scourge*. But, of course, your mileage may vary.

So far as standalone fantasy novels go, *The Scourge* is a solid new entry from Jennifer A. Nielsen. It's not life-changing, but the threads of friendship and the hilarity of Ani's narration should please even the most jaded of cynics... myself included.

Rating: 7 out of 10.

Fruitcakes and Gimchi in SPAAACE

YOON HA LEE

ONCE UPON A TIME, I read a science fiction novel by Elizabeth Moon in which one of the plot points revolved around a fruitcake. (I'm not naming the novel because this is a bit of a spoiler, but if you've read it, you'll recognize it.) I have heard stories of fruitcakes, mostly lamenting their bricklike texture and lack of flavor. Indeed, part of the plot point hinged on the reader being aware of this common judgment of fruitcakes.

I'm not knocking the book! It was a hilarious plot point and I roared when I saw how cleverly Moon had worked it in. But it did make me think: Why couldn't I put Korean food into my science fiction, instead of familiar Western foods? And so, when I wrote my space opera *Ninefox Gambit*, which takes place in a secondary world populated by cockamamie Asians, I decided that my space forces were going to flit around the galaxy serving gimchi to their troops. (Alas, the gimchi is not a clever plot point. It's just background food culture.)

My earlier sf/f stories drew on Western culture and history because the sf/f I read growing up did, and I was emulating the models in front of me. To be sure, I'd run into occasional exceptions, some problematic, some less so. I'd enjoyed Raymond E. Feist and Janny Wurts' Empire trilogy and Geraldine Harris's Seven Citadels quartet. Even so, it took years for me to see that I had other alternatives.

I spent half my childhood in South Korea, and eventually it occurred to me that I could mine this for world-building purposes, even if I didn't formally study any Korean history until college. Prof. Barry S. Strauss's course on War and Diplomacy on the Korean Peninsula, covering both the Imjin War and the Korean War, proved too good to resist. This may be the Korean in me speaking, but as far as storytelling drama goes, it's almost impossible to improve on the Imjin War. You have Admiral Yi Sun-Shin, undefeated at sea, who is thrown in jail and tortured despite his victories thanks to political intrigues. You have the *gisaeng* (artisan-entertainer women, similar to Japanese geisha) Nongae, who lured a Japanese general to a cliff and flung herself over the edge with him, killing them both. You have the Battle of Myeongnyang, in which Admiral Yi defeated the Japanese navy while outnumbered ten to one. If science fiction had its far future Roman analogues and samurai analogues, why not Joseon Korea analogues? And so I wrote "Between Two Dragons," a what-if based loosely on the Imjin War and the question of Yi's stubborn loyalty; and later, "The Battle of Candle Arc," whose tactics are based on the tactics at Myeongnyang.

Part of my motivation for using Myeongnyang was selfish. It's an example of a spectacular underdog victory that Western readers wouldn't necessarily be familiar with. That's not a criticism of people who didn't know about it. I didn't know about the specific battle until college, although I'd grown up with vague stories about Admiral Yi, and I *lived* in Korea before then! (Ironically, I spent my high school years reading military history, all right—I read Caesar, Tacitus, and Josephus.) But it felt so freeing when I realized that I didn't have to be limited to the history I had learned in school—largely Western military history—for inspiration.

There's nothing particularly special about Korean military history. It just happens to be a corner of the world I'm familiar with thanks to family and having lived in the country. But the world is a big place. Just as reading fantasy inspired my interest in trebuchets and Cannae and Vegetius, I hope that I'll see more sf/f drawing upon a greater variety of histories and cultures.

In Her Head, In Her Eyes

YUKIMI OGAWA

TRILLS OF SILVER, TRILLS OF blue.

She wanted to watch on. She wanted to remember them, wanted to make them her own. But soon, too soon, she was pulled up, back into the air, where she had to fight for breath, fight to be on her feet.

She hit the hard workshop floor, heavy head first. Though her head was protected, she cried out anyway. Slowly, she raised herself up and tried to glare at them, all of them standing around the stale pot of unused indigo dye in which they had just tried to drown her. Most of them kept laughing at her, but a few seemed to sense her unseen glare, and backed off warily.

Then, a voice from the entrance to the workshop. "What is going on in here?"

The bullies scattered instantly at the voice's calm authority. Everyone knew who commanded that voice, just as everyone knew he was the only person who would dare stand up for the strange new servant. Drenched in old dye, the servant girl shifted and dipped her heavy head, and busied herself squeezing her sleeves. Slowly the owner of the voice walked in, frowning. "Hase. I told you to come or call for me when in trouble. Are you all right?"

Hase bowed as low as she could, unbalanced with the substantial weight atop her head. "Yes. I appreciate our young master's concern."

The young man—the third noble son of the family of artisan dyers—knelt before her. "Hase," he said. "You must tell them they'll be in trouble if they do anything to you. Use my name. Who were they?" He was the only person in the entire house who called her by her real name and not Pot Head.

"Again, I appreciate my master's concern," Hase said, "but in truth, I am fine. And here, my robe—now it's dyed in indigo and looks pretty!"

Still kneeling, the young man grinned. "You smiled. At last!"

Hase hurriedly composed herself and looked down. Suddenly she was aware of how her robe was clinging to her skin, how the blue-black pungent water was running down her dark hair, down her torso, how quickly the warm dye was starting to cool off. "Young master, this is not a place for a noble. I must tidy myself up now."

"Yes. Be sure to keep yourself warm."

Hase bowed again, watching the young man leave before standing and rushing abruptly to the servants quarters in search of solitude and warmth.

No one knew why Hase wore a pot on her head. No one in the noble house, in the region, had even seen the materials from which the pot was made. *It must be some sort of iron,* people would whisper marveling at the reflective surface shining brightly as a mirror in the space where her eyes should be. No one had ever seen Hase's eyes, or anything behind the pot's smooth countenance--only her nose and mouth were visible below its cold protective edge.

Since her arrival at the house, of course many had tried to rip the pot form her head, but to no avail. The pot, so closely fitted to Hase's skull, would not, could not come off. Yet others tried to crack it open to reveal the girl beneath, but no tool could do it any damage. Eventually, they all gave up.

The only thing anyone knew about Hase for certain was that she came from The Island—a fabled place, far away from their shores. Even nobles, such as the ones who owned this fine home, were not rich enough to travel to The Island. How pot-covered Hase ended up here, people could only speculate.

Beyond the metallic pot concealing her head, Hase appeared perfectly plain, which only added to the mystery surrounding her. The people of Hase's Island were rumored to be great beauties, with skin and hair and eyes of all colors: hues of flowers and jewels, of stars and sunsets. Some, it was rumored, even bore patterns on their skin—-not tattooed or painted on, but opalescent designs born from the womb. It was common knowledge that everyone from the Island was beautiful, inspiring poetry and art, stories and dreams.

Only look at Hase. She had ordinary skin just like everyone else, without a single shocking color or pattern to be seen. Her hair was thick, beautiful and dark as a crow's wing, but perfectly ordinary. So no one in the household, neither noble nor servant, believed her claim as to her birthplace--no one, that is, save the family's third son.

A few nights after her arrival at the house, Sai visited Hase's makeshift cot inside the storehouse. At first she shied away, thinking he had come to take advantage of her. But he waved his hand dismissively and sat down by the door, leaving it fully open. There was no light inside, for no fire was allowed in the storehouse; only moonlight illuminated the room, spilling through the door and reflecting off her potted head.

Sai gestured towards the moon. "Look at how beautiful the moon is here, without all the lights of the house. Don't be greedy and keep it all to yourself!"

Slowly, Hase closed the distance to the door where he was, her thin blanket wrapped tightly around her body. She peered at him cautiously, the starry night reflecting in the cool metal of her gaze. "We have a pond of the color of moonlight," she said quietly.

"On your island? Where they say everyone is beautiful?"

"There is no such place where everyone is beautiful. People always try to find the flaws and imperfections in all things. On my island, there are other plain things. As plain as Hase appears here." She bowed her spherical heavy head and clutched her blanket tighter around her.

"And the pot..."

"It has nothing to do with Hase's island, master." Hase gave her heavy head a little shake.

The young man nodded. He looked as though he had more things he wanted to ask, but said no more and looked on at the moon.

Unlike the younger servants, the adults didn't quite bully Hase, though no one seemed to like her much. They knew a certain amount of money had been exchanged for her service, enough of a sum to make them believe that she must be from the Island and that she genuinely must want to work under the dye masters. Still, among any of the servants, any kindness towards Hase remained to be seen. For when Hase, dripping with old indigo dye and shivering, finally made her way to the servants' quarters to ask for towels, she found little sympathy. The elder dye master, Hase's superior, simply wrinkled her nose and dropped the towels at Hase's feet. "For once, just have a bath. I can't let you serve at the meeting tonight in that state, and we can't spare a hand."

"What meeting?"

"You don't notice anything, do you?" the woman sighed. "The eldest and the middle brothers' wives and other relatives are coming to visit."

Hase tilted her heavy head to one side in question. "What about the third brother's wife?"

"You know he doesn't have a wife yet," the dye master snorted. "If he did we'd all have stopped him before he went into that storehouse your first night to have you."

Hase stared blankly at the dye master, smooth impassive metal reflecting the older woman's sneer, until the dye master shooed her away.

Hase didn't have much time to enjoy the bath. Soon the relatives started to arrive, and she was herded along with the other servants, bustling tea and refreshments to the family. All the relatives openly stared at Hase and the smooth pot covering her head, mouths agape at her strangeness. *Pot Head*, they whispered behind her back, quickly picking up the servants' name for her. The wives of the first and second brothers took great delight in her peculiar appearance, laughing at her gleaming helmet of metal. The elder wife quickly tired of the game and Hase's calm, and exclaimed, "Why, I hate her face!"

"But she doesn't have a face!" The younger wife laughed even harder than before.

"I hate that she doesn't. We are laughing at her and she should be angry, or embarrassed at the very least! Look at her, with her stupid mouth, her tiny nose." The elder wife gestured rudely at Hase, trying to engage the servant. "The only parts of her face you can see, and she has no reaction."

Hase bowed as gracefully as she could in the style of her fellow servants, the movement awkward in many ways. The angle of her neck and back were tilted just wrong, the speed with which she retreated to the more comfortable, upright position to alleviate the weight of her head a little too fast. The jerky movements only fueled the younger wife's amusement, her laughter renewed with malicious glee.

"Oh Pot Head, heavy-head, just try not to get in our way!" The younger wife pushed Hase by the pot on her head, cackling harder still when Hase fell to the wooden floor with a dull thud, potted-head first.

Slowly, slowly, Hase dragged herself up onto her feet, as she heard the two wives walk away, laughing and laughing.

Both wives and their husbands were young and relatively newly-wed, and the two women measured themselves against each other in every regard. They compared their wedding gifts and the favor of their new parents-in-law; they compared their best robes, their skills in music and poetry. Every day and every night, the wives would compare their positions, while their men drank sake, the women tea, and a steady barrage of refreshments flew from the kitchens into their mouths.

All the while, Hase lurked in the background, her domed, impassive head missing not a single detail. From the hallways and the corners of each room, Hase stole glimpses of the fine embroidery of the women's robes, fascinated by the expensive, exquisite artifacts that shimmered in the wives' hands.

One day, the elder wife caught Hase staring at her robe and sneered, her venomous glare focused on Hase's reflective helmet. Hase shivered, transfixed by the wife's disdain, unable to look or move away.

"Here." Sai handed her a bundle. "Of all the gifts the women brought, these were the only things my relatives weren't much keen on. I'm sure you can have it."

Hase opened the bundle, and found two spindles of fine gold and silver threads. She turned the spools in her hands, feeling the fine filigree of each thread, and sighed. "These must be expensive enough that someone may like to save for later use. Is it certain that Hase can have it?"

"We are dye masters here, not for embroidery or even weaving." Sai smiled at Hase encouragingly. "But you like patterns, I've heard? That's why you've come all the way here, isn't it?"

"Yes." She nodded, a slow, languid inclination of her heavy, masked head. "On my island, we need more colors, more patterns. Patterns, especially, to be reflected on the beloved children of the Island. I must study."

"You mean you can decide what colors and patterns your babies will bear?" Sai leaned forward eagerly.

"No, sir. We create new patterns, we discover more colors, but our goddess alone can decide. We all wish to please our goddess."

Sai frowned, confused. Hase almost smiled at that.

After a moment of silence, she said quietly, "These look as though they represent the young wives themselves. They are so different and yet, they go so well with each other."

Sai, leaning in closer to hear her better, laughed. "Are you being sarcastic?"

"No, sir! They are lovely, those two."

She had said this a little louder, but still, the third son did not lean back. She knew what that meant. And though everything was awkward with her heavy pot, the hard wooden ground, the thin futon, this time Hase smiled. The pot weighed her down, pinned her to the floor, as if Sai's eyes intent on her covered face weren't enough to affix her there already.

When she was alone again, Hase pulled the spindles Sai had given her out from the folds of her sleeves. She placed them on the ground beside her futon, then changed her mind and put them on the pillow and carefully laid her heavy head beside them. The two colors filled her reflected sight, shimmering and twining in cruel beauty, fueling rather than smothering her desire.

The next day, Hase walked dreamily through the dyed cloths fluttering in the wind, being dried. Some bore glue for patterns to be washed away later, and some still had strings marking the fabric for simpler patterns. A few plain cloths with no patters at all fluttered alongside these elaborate designs, forming a small sea of color and texture upon which Hase and her metal potted head were afloat. Her heavy head swiveled in wonder, slowly, taking in all of the colors and styles. She had to memorize all these patterns, for the dye masters would never teach her how to make them. The blues. The whites. Everything in between. But just then she heard a voice, interrupting her quiet study. "You seem to have had a very good time last night."

Startled, Hase spun around, searching for the source of the voice though she already knew its owner. She walked on in between the waves of cloths, currents and bubbles, seaweeds of patterns, towards the voice. At the end of the last row, she found her.

Hase bowed as well as she could, and asked: "Was that statement aimed at me, mistress?"

Trills of blue, a line of silver. For a moment, the older of the two wives—the one Hase called in her mind Silver—looked away from her. "Why did you come here? What is it you want from us?"

"I come to learn about dyeing..."

"Oh do you? So seducing our brother-in-law was part of your plan?"

Hase shook her head; that was all she could do.

"With a face like yours it must be really easy to lie, isn't it? Are you even really from that Island everybody's talking about? Does it even exist? Did you think looking ordinary would make us feel you're one of us, or did you think we'd be too easy to deceive, so you didn't bother mocking those colors and patterns of the Island's people?" The elder wife's anger and spite burned in her eyes.

Involuntarily, Hase raised her hand through Silver's tirade, resting it gently over a nearby cloth and marveling at its fine knots and textures. She tried to imagine the pattern the knots might make eventually, and failed. "My patterns, I guess, are in my head."

Silver frowned. "In your head? What are you talking about?"

Hase stroked the cloth again, trying to coax the pattern into life. "Yes. I'm the head pattern designer of my clan, as I have told the great mistress here." She recalled Sai's mother in her finest robes, her eyes cold as she assessed Hase and her claims. "I have to extract the patterns from my head, and to do that, I need to know more ways to express the patterns, of course!" Hase's voice rose in pitch, in eagerness and fervor. Her potted head glittered in the sunlight. "But, but the people in this region, especially the dye masters wouldn't allow the dye or dyeing methods out of the region. We—my aunts and other guardians and I, of course, of course—had to promise I wouldn't take any—*any!*—indigo out of this place when we arranged my apprenticeship here! But nobody can prevent me from taking these blues and whites and everything else with me inside my head! And...what is the matter?"

Silver had backed away from Hase, the hate in her eyes faded into wariness and fear at Hase's rambling outburst.

At Silver's discomfort, Hase immediately reverted to her usual quiet demeanor. "Forgive me, I shouldn't have kept our young mistress standing here, listening to Hase's useless babblings! Did I answer the question well enough?"

Silver shook her head. "I...no. Not at all. Now, there are only more questions than before."

"Forgive me, mistress. Please, pardon my rudeness!"

"Don't." Silver raised a hand towards Hase, who had just taken one step closer to her. "Come no closer. And don't you dare look at me like that."

"Like what, mistress?"

But Silver just waved her hand and walked away in a flutter of silk, leaving Hase standing amid the sea of patterned cloth, her face as smooth and impassive as ever.

Sai's words were always gentle. Hase felt as though she could fall asleep listening to him.

"Is it true," the young man asked, waking her up out from her reverie, "that on the Island, some people change their colors as they grow old? I heard that from one of the relatives; they'd heard that somewhere along the trip here."

Hase inclined her potted head. "Some do, yes. I know a person whose eyes changed from light green to viridian, yellow, and eventually brown, like leaves. They crumbled in the end, and the person went blind."

"Oh. I'm sorry to hear that."

"That person knew what was going to happen and worked hard to prepare for it. It's not that bad, when things are predictable like that."

After a while he sighed. "I cannot imagine the life of your people."

"There is no need, sir."

"But I want to. I want to know more about you."

Hase turned from Sai and remained silent, playing with the twines of silver and gold spindles he had given her.

In her eyes she wove her patterns of gold and silver. With occasional blue that punctuated the new design, it shaped hearts and veins.

But then, just before she could wholly grasp the new pattern, her heavy head was yanked back as another pair of hands held onto her shoulders. Her shoulders ached under the hands' vice-like grip, pain blossoming in sharp edges and radiating from her chest. And yet, despite the ache, Hase felt the most the bitter edge of frustration at losing the pattern she had been imagining, weaving in her eyes.

Below her, Hase could see a large basin of water as the pair of hands holding her shoulders yanked backwards further and the other hands pulling at the pot on her head went the other direction. She coughed, and heard a young servant's voice: "Mistress, if we go any further she might be sick, or even, she might die. I wouldn't be able to explain to our masters what happened, if asked."

"Simple, tell them you punished her because she had stolen the gold and silver threads." Silver's calm voice. "If she dies, it's an accident."

She'd have preferred drowning in the dye pot, especially now with the new indigo being brewed, the bubbles from fermentation slowly blooming like a nebula over the dark liquid. But that would spoil the new dye. Through the pain she imagined the dye's warmth, the smell, explosion of stars as the liquid rushed into her head. Hase shivered.

Behind her, the younger of the wives burst out laughing, her voice full of gold dust. "Then let me do it! I want to choke her with my own hands!"

Silver glowered at Gold. "Are you stupid? We cannot do it ourselves. We are going to say that the servant did it to impress us, of their own will. Be careful not to get your robe wet or touch anything that could prove we were here."

At that, the servant boy's hands loosened a little from Hase's shoulders. Hase whimpered, as she heard Gold make a frustrated noise.

"Anyway." Silver came around to where Hase could see her, and crouched down to flash the two spindles of thread. "These are confiscated. You don't need them, anyway, do you? Because the patterns are all in your head, like you said."

"No! Please, I need them! They are my inspiration!"

Silver smiled her cold, cold smile. Hase tried to reach out for the spindles, but the servant boy pulled her back. She heard Gold laughing again, saw Silver tuck the spindles into her sleeve.

Hase could feel her aunts' frustration. She wasn't making enough progress. Seeing the color of indigo change in impossible gradation, learning simple knots that revealed unexpected patterns weren't enough yet for her to create new, satisfying designs. She needed inspiration, and it seemed as though the people here were determined to snatch away that inspiration just when she thought she had found it.

Until one night, at the far end of the house, where she found the three young nobles.

She watched as they tangled and disentangled, making new patterns for her every second. The unreliable screen of organdy, which they must have chosen so that they _would_ be seen, provided her with even more inspirations, as it swayed and added a sheen to their passion. Patterns, patterns, patterns.

"What is it that we don't have and the pot girl does?" Silver's cool voice carried through the night as she gracefully moved to ride the man.

"The pot hides her face and let me see my own lovely self on it," Sai said breezily. Gold sighed with pleasure behind them.

"And also," he said, pushing up a little to grab at Silver's buttocks, "she is from an island full of treasures. Why not make her a slave of mine, let her serve as a liaison between us and the Island?"

"Did you say 'us'?" Gold crawled up from behind Sai and kissed him upside down.

"Besides." Sai lay fully down again and reached out to touch Gold now. "She looks ordinary, I mean, apart from that pot, but who knows what her children will look like? I know her aunts have the colors, because she told just to me, because she trusts me, so why not her children?"

"So then you can sell them?"

"Or we could give them to the high generals or perhaps even the Emperor!"

The three all laughed. Then Silver said, while Gold's laughing voice was still trilling in the air: "How did you make her trust you? She doesn't have a face, it's hard to tell what she thinks. Even if you're good at putting up with your own face staring back at you."

"Oh, that was easy. Just being kind to her is more than enough. Treat her as a woman, as no one else does around here. And she's yours."

Gold laughed. Sai chuckled. Silver grinned and licked her lips as she cast her glance upward. "Really? If that's true, you must be a very, very undemanding person, aren't you, Pot Head?"

Sai followed Silver's eyes. Hase, previously hidden in the dimness of the corridor behind the screen, stepped into the light and moaned softly, her sigh swaying the cotton organdy in front of her. Sai bolted upright, pushing Silver off him. "Hase!"

Silver let out a laugh, a trilling of cold, cruel bells. "Oh, Sai, didn't you know she uses this path to get to that stupid cot of hers in the storehouse? You should have paid more attention! If you intended to fool her long enough so that she would take you to that stupid Island, that is!"

Sai looked embarrassed, seemed to be searching for the right words. But soon he gave up, knowing there were no right words to save face with Hase. He looked at her mouth, her smooth, potted head and spoke. "Yes, I was using you, but you had to know this. Why else would I, a man with a rank, place special favor upon an odd girl like you if it weren't to use you?"

None of the three could read Hase's face, of course, with that mirrored helmet of hers. But they could see her shaking. Silver and Gold looked pleased. Sai still looked a little embarrassed, a little uncertain, despite his declaration.

"So why don't we make a child here?" Gold said.

Taking that as invitation, Hase stepped over the threshold, pushing the organdy out of the way. "But why? Why are you so interested in me?" she asked.

Sai frowned. "No, I told you, I'm more interested in your..."

But Hase wasn't listening to him. She crouched down, not to face him, but to face Silver beside him. "You are like a cold fire that seeks to burn me out."

Silver's grin became wider. "Of course, I hate you, your pot, your behavior, your strangeness—"

"Am I? Am I strange enough? Everybody says I'm plain, with my ordinary hair, my ordinary skin, my plain colors. Everybody's disappointed!"

"What?"

She turned to Sai. "And to you, yes, I don't mind having your genes. We always need more variations."

"We...what?"

Hase moved on her hands and knees, scampering towards Gold. "Oh, I love the way you laugh. Like gold dust exploding and filling the space. Laugh! Laugh, laugh, laugh at me!"

By then, even Gold was frowning with discomfort, and the silence drew out between the four.

"You are disgusting," Silver spat, breaking the quiet.

"Yes!" Hase turned around to her. "Yes, I'm disgusting! I love being bullied! I love being punished! Bully me! Punish me! You like it too, don't you!"

The three young people slowly backed away from Hase. She swiveled her heavy smooth head back and forth between Silver and Gold—Sai was no use now for her, not paying enough attention to her and therefore, misunderstanding her. Of course, in retrospect, all the questions he had asked her were about the Island, not Hase herself. Gold was nicely cruel, but she was more like a small child, always looking for a new toy. She'd probably tire of Hase sooner or later. So she looked at Silver, whose hateful stare almost choked Hase, like a flood of warm indigo dye.

Trills of silver, quiver of gold.

"Aunts," Hase whispered, grinning impossibly wide, resembling a huge-headed, one-eye monster. "I finally found what I needed. My offering to our goddess!"

Silver backed further away on her hands and buttocks, eyes shining with fear. Her terror made a sharp pang run through Hase, a shiver that wove new patterns, a shiver that pierced colorful stitches over her bright darkness, her white-out canvas.

Silver winced at her own reflection on the mirror of Hase's helmet; what she didn't, couldn't know was that it was a mirror both outside and inside alike. The inner mirror was always connected to the server, where her aunts received and observed every pattern Hase formed. The outer mirror projected and transferred information of outside world onto Hase's brain, in the place of her long-crumbled eyes. Pains and hurts, both physical and psychological, inspired her more than anything; they had known that much through years of observation. That was why her aunts had sent her to this strangely feudal place--as much for the pain as for the rare colors and dyes that weren't allowed to be exported.

"I'm the head designer of the clan, you see," Hase said, smiling her eye-less, reflective smile. "We need more patterns, colors shapes to satisfy our goddess. Favor of our goddess means wealth, and wealth means we will be able to afford a more expensive, lighter-smaller-better helmet for me. But if you prefer me in this heavy old thing, if you'd bully me more in this thing, I want to keep wearing it forever!"

Hase's breath came in quick pants of arousal and excitement, while Silver's breathing turned ragged with terror. Hase could hear Gold making strange noises, like choking, like gagging, like she was about to vomit. No noise, no move could be heard from Sai. *Has he fainted?* Hase queried halfheartedly. *Useless youngest boy.*

"What do you want?" Silver choked out.

Hase shifted into a *seiza* position. "I want you inside my helmet." She thought for a split second, and then, waved her hands in excited denial. "Not you, but the copy of your mental map, so that you'd keep on inspiring me." She stopped her hands and placed them on her chest, and crooned, "Yes, those eyes. I want your eyes, spiteful, hateful, always on me. Don't worry, it won't hurt you!"

"I don't understand." Silver backed away further, frantically looking for an exit. "If I let you do that, you will leave us alone?"

Hase's cheeks and lips were enough to tell Silver that the pot headed girl was disappointed. "I thought you wanted to keep me around, to hate me, to laugh at me. But yes, if you let me have your copy, I'd simply go home with it. And I'll send you treasures with the patterns you inspired, if you'd like that."

Quietly, slowly, as to not startle Hase into excitement again, Silver shifted to sit cross-legged. "Do send them, then. You are going to be rich, right? Why not us, too?" Silver's eyes turned calculating, momentarily forgetting her fear.

Hase grinned wide again. Behind them Gold started to sob. "Sister, no! What if she's lying about not hurting you?"

"I am *not!*" Hase whipped her large head back, wobbling slightly, making Gold jump. "It's just like... drawing a picture of her! Surely you've been drawn a portrait before? A beautiful person like you? Did it hurt you, ever?"

"N-no, but..."

"I'm all right," Silver said. "She looks much more interested in being hurt, rather than hurting people, anyway."

Hase nodded eagerly.

Silver said, "All the beautiful things sent from her are mine, then."

Hase slowly lifted the helmet, the mirror in front of her eyes.

Gold couldn't see what her sister-in-law saw, but she saw Silver's incomprehension as she took in whatever lay beyond the girl's helmet, and began to scream. Silver screamed on, and on, until she lost all her breath, until her throat started to bleed.

Until her sanity was lost.

Apathy seized Sai after Pot Head disappeared, people concluded. As for the two young wives, no one could determine what caused their sad turn of situation. The older one kept her eyes open unseeing, her lips slightly parted but always unspeaking--and when she saw something beautiful, anything remotely beautiful, she'd start to scream anew. The family decided to keep her in a white-walled room with plain white doors, where she was always dressed in coarse linen robes without design, color or pattern. The younger wife fared a little better than her sister-in-law, but not by much. She wouldn't leave Silver's side, sometimes crying loudly like a small girl, sometimes giggling hysterically, especially when anyone ever tried to detach her from her sister. But she took care of Silver and of herself without problem, so people decided to keep her in the white room, too.

People laughed at Sai and despised him for his laziness. They treated the women as if they didn't exist, and the first and the second brothers of the house remarried. The white room became a small fish bone stuck in the household's throat; it hurts and you want to get rid of it, but it might hurt even worse if you try to force it out.

There are things people don't forget. Things like the way the people of the house mistreated the strange woman from the Island with her heavy, potted head. Things like how, eventually, the hired woman disappeared, and all those close her were driven to madness. No one wanted to go near the family after that.

Slowly, the once prosperous house decayed.

It happened on a crisp autumn day, the clouds high, the air thin, the cold enfolding the quiet, decaying house. It arrived, alone, bearing nothing. It walked through the people who gazed, who gaped. Without searching or asking or even hesitating, it walked into the house, towards the white room. And it opened the white doors.

It was a child.

Its hair was indigo, its eyes the color of young leaves. Its face—every surface of its skin—bore intricate patterns, woven with silver, gold, and every shade of indigo. It was a thing of beauty framed in the whiteness of the room.

No one had to ask; the two women recognized it as soon as they saw it. It was Hase's creation.

"I have come, to be yours," the child said.

The women started to scream.

Characters Are Not A Coloring Book: Or, Why the Black Hermione is a Poor Apology for the Ingrained Racism of Harry Potter

MIMI MONDAL

LIKE MANY PEOPLE OF MY generation, I grew up on *Harry Potter*. As an introverted, class-topping little girl, I identified hardcore with Hermione Granger. I had sorted myself into a House (Slytherin, unfortunately) long before there was Pottermore. I had all the spells at the tip of my tongue, just as I knew all the minor characters, subplots and plot holes by heart. My best friend was a *Harry Potter* fanfic writer for years, and although I never wrote any fanfic myself, the online Harry Potter communities were my first experience of fandom, which was my first experience of LiveJournal, which in turn was my first experience of the international SFF community.

I wrote J.K. Rowling a snail-mail letter, addressed to the Bloomsbury office in London, when she killed off Sirius Black in *The Order of the Phoenix*, telling her how that was uncool and, frankly, here's a list of *much better things* she could've done with the story instead. I was one of the kids who felt entitled to tell Rowling off on such matters, because I knew about *Harry Potter* as much as anyone possibly could; because I had speculated about possible futures of the story more than she herself may have (ha!); because *Harry Potter* was a core part of my childhood… and how could she just have casually violated that? (Or no, "felt entitled" would be the wrong description, because no one ever *feels entitled* to do anything. The best part about the entitled is that they *feel offended* by other people doing their thing, which they refuse to believe *can* rightfully be those other people's thing to do.)

I have felt as possessive about the *Harry Potter* canon as anyone I've ever met, so once again, when people are talking about Noma Dumezweni being cast as the adult Hermione, and the possibility that Hermione may not have been white in the first place, I can feel my (non-existent) entitlement begin to tickle. I have always been Hermione among my friends; it's the rare character in which I saw myself reflected, validated in fiction; the character whose triumphs and losses were my own—surely no one else can have the last word on whether a black Hermione "feels right"? If it doesn't feel right *to me*, there's no way that can be retconned into the canon. That's violating my childhood. I won't have it.

Except that I was never a white girl myself. Through all my childhood years of hardcore Pottermania, I was a brown girl growing up in Calcutta, India.

Growing up in Calcutta in the early 2000s, identifying with fictional characters was a relatively simple thing. Unlike children of color in Western countries who clearly experience their minority status, I grew up surrounded by other Indians. We had our Indian books and films, sometimes in our native languages, in which everyone was Indian; and then we had our foreign books and films, in which *no one* was Indian. And, in a smaller city like Calcutta, we hardly met any white people, so there was no paradigm in which we felt *unmistakeably different* from them. White people were allegorical, just like fairies or anthropomorphized animals were allegorical. My friends and I had no problem identifying with Cinderella, Peter Pan, Elizabeth Bennet, Sherlock Holmes, or any other white character that we read. Each of us had a *Friends* protagonist that we identified with, a Backstreet Boy or a Spice Girl that was SO us, so it was only natural that everyone was a *Harry Potter* character as well.

As an adult, I have learned there were larger dynamics to this placid identification—the way we Indians, or South Asians, see ourselves as a minority at all; the way British colonization had treated us, which was very different from the way colonial subjects were treated in Africa or elsewhere in the world. Of all the races of color, we South Asians probably speak the most "flawless" English. We still proudly brandish our British laws, British institutions, British way of life—among them, elite boarding schools and school uniforms, just like Hogwarts. Our greatest class aspiration is to be able to pass as just-slightly-darker white people. During my stays as an adult in the UK and the USA, I've found my fellow South Asians largely reluctant to identify as a community with black,

Latinx, or (non-south) Asian people. My fellow South Asians refuse to "see color", as if only if we do it collectively and hard enough, color will also refuse to see us.

Not seeing color was the way I was brought up, and a large part of not seeing color is to get uncomfortable and gently sidestep the people and texts that *do* see color. People who don't see color are usually a more benign lot than outright racists—they're "well-intentioned", if anything. It wasn't like I *never* encountered any text with a mixed-race cast of characters, but I didn't know how to engage with them, so I didn't. The rare white-authored texts with substantial Indian characters, nearly always portrayed with ignorance and bias, I put aside as books that I didn't like very much—*The Jungle Book* and *Kim* by Rudyard Kipling, *A Passage to India* by E.M. Forster, *The City of Joy* by Dominique Lapierre. I was cool with *Twenty Thousand Leagues Under the Sea*, in which Captain Nemo is an Indian man, but his race doesn't affect anything else in the story. Or *Wuthering Heights*, where there's a tiny suggestion that Heathcliff may have been an Indian prince, but ditto for the rest.

This adamant refusal to see color is the reason why I didn't feel awkward with *Harry Potter* at the age when I started reading it; the reason why I can no longer read it without cringing. And color isn't even the only thing that *Harry Potter* refuses to see. Sexuality, religion—you name it. *Harry Potter* isn't an offensive text, but it's equally inoffensive to the homophobic, xenophobic readers. And maybe those are the things that we need to talk about, when we are shocked that the fandom we loved so much as children also managed to nurture the people who are so hateful towards our mere existence.

The inescapable fact is that most minorities never really did exist in *Harry Potter*, except in a tokenistic way, or retconned into the narrative afterwards. Much before the controversy over the black Hermione, there was the controversy over the gay Dumbledore—one that played out pretty much along the same lines. Nothing in the books suggests that Dumbledore *couldn't* have been gay, but nothing in them actually establishes, leave alone defends, his homosexuality either. You can read the vaguest hints of a homoerotic friendship with Grindelwald, but the fan-fiction community had been shipping everyone with everyone else for years, and I can never be sure of what might have been an *intended* hint in the books. (Sirius Black and James Potter were definitely homoerotic too, right? Non?) In the actual books, Dumbledore was just the generic unpartnered male. I'd have never known, if I didn't read the "official" announcement on Rowling's website, that she intended him to be gay.

Nor would I have suspected that she intended Dean Thomas to be black, until I watched the first movie. Dean morphed early enough, and remained insignificant enough since then, for not many fans to object to his non-whiteness (his biggest function in the books being dating Ginny Weasley, and getting dumped at a convenient enough point for Harry to present himself as the superior alternative). The same goes for Angelina Johnson, who doesn't have *any* function at all, despite being a kickass Quidditch player, captain, and rudimentary feminist.

Who are the other children of color at Hogwarts? Lee Jordan, with his dreadlocks and distinct Caribbean vibe, the cheerful black friend whose only talent is to comment on the microphone with a blind, almost comical, allegiance for the side he supports. Lee is a prankster and *almost* an accomplice of Fred and George Weasley, but never entirely; he isn't welcomed into the family like Ron's friends are. Blaise Zabini, as one of the beta readers of this essay pointed out, and I won't be surprised if you hadn't noticed either, because it wasn't ever mentioned in the books. Cho Chang—Harry's first love interest, a name that had struck me as a pleasant surprise when I first read it, and who was played by a Chinese actor in the movies (a fact that we should be thankful about, it seems, considering the rampant whitewashing of characters of color all over SFF filmmaking), and who conveniently doesn't do a single thing in the books that a white girl wouldn't. Parvati and Padma Patil—fraternal (originally identical) twins, each in a different house, which could have been *such* an interesting plot device, but instead their greatest achievement is to be Harry and Ron's reluctant and eventually exasperating dates to the Yule Ball. And what the actual fuck were those Yule Ball costumes? Remind me to never shop at the charity store that *those* travesties came from.[1]

Fun trivia: Ever notice that *not even a single time* are the words "Chinese" and "Indian" used in the *Harry Potter* books? Not even to describe food, leace alone these actual characters. (What would the British do without Chinese or Indian food?! But no—no one in *Harry Potter* eats anything apart from the standard pub cuisine.) Bet you didn't.

No one in *Harry Potter* speaks a different language, or even a broken English, apart from the Europeans—the French and Bulgarian school contingents; the German wandmaker. No prizes for guessing that we never run into Cho's or the Patil sisters' parents casually on Diagon Alley. Their parents are all Muggles anyway, right? Because if they weren't, Rowling would have to deal with the possibility of non-white, non-English magic, which she has started acknowledging *only recently* with Native-American magic in North America, and already managed to make a number of people unhappy. Dean's father wasn't a Muggle, but he was also conveniently swiped off "in the war", and Dean brought up by a Muggle mother and stepfather, so that we don't have to bother our-

1 A fact that Buzzfeed India Editor-in-chief Rega Jha elucidates on to great length in "Let's Never Forgive the Grave Injustice of Padma and Parvati's Yule Ball Outfits", *Buzzfeed*, 3 March 2016. Accessed from https://www.buzzfeed.com/regajha/harry-potter-and-the-prisoners-of-bad-fashion?utm_term=.ynrQDva9j#.gvDaAv3qJ on 31 July 2016.

selves with black-people magic either. At least one of Blaise's parents (or an earlier ancestor) should be black, but we never learn whether it is the famously beautiful witch who has been widowed seven times, or one of the unfortunate deceased, since we have no idea about Blaise's race (or even his gender) for most of the series, even though a non-white pureblood Muggle-hating Slytherin should've been a damn interesting character in this world, again.

No one in *Harry Potter* is Muslim or Jewish, and I'm beginning to think that's because these communities are stereotyped as being more rigorous about their religious identities than Hindus or the Chinese. What *is* the stand on religion in the British wizarding community, anyway? Why do they hold those Christmas celebrations at Hogwarts—opulent enough, only without any explicit religious ceremony—but there's never any Eid, Passover, Diwali, Chinese New Year?

My problem with *Harry Potter* is that *only the white people win*, or rather, no one who wins is of any other race, which is exactly the kind of pattern that colorblindness convinces us not to see. The people of color in *Harry Potter* aren't villains either, they're just overall nobody important—annoying dates, unsatisfactory boyfriends, and maybe some of you even remember the part in *The Order of the Phoenix* where Harry described kissing Cho as snogging with a hosepipe? No matter that that girl had recently lost her boyfriend (also a white hero, of course), and maybe that confused rebound was the only reason she ever agreed to get together with Harry. In a world where everyone is falling over each other to get Harry Potter's attention, somehow a girl who isn't hysteric about Harry Potter but still chooses to treat him with consideration isn't worth praising for her clearsightedness at all. She's only depicted in detail in *The Order of the Phoenix*, and only as the girl who just can't shut up about her now-inconsequential heartbreak and accept that she's leveled up by nabbing the mighty Harry Potter. (And, of course, Harry gets to dump her. That's totally not contradictory to the earlier detail that Cho had hardly ever given him the time of day before she was cracked open emotionally by the death of Cedric Diggory and the return of Voldemort. Because in what world does a woman of color get to reject a white-hero paramour? She should be grateful that the white guy deigned to be romantically interested in her at all. Damn, so liberal, that guy!)

My problem with *Harry Potter* is that the Dursley family, despicable characters beyond doubt, are never seen to complain about their Pakistani neighbors, although they are *exactly* the kind of people who complain about their Pakistani neighbors, the kind of people who hurl "Paki" at every brown person as if that's an insult, the kind of people who vote for Brexit or Making America Great Again. (One in every twenty people in the UK is a person of South Asian descent.[2] There are very few white people *anywhere* on that island who don't have a South Asian neighbor. Some small town in Surrey, within commuting distance of London? There should probably be more South Asians living there than there would be whites!) But no, the objects of the Dursleys' scorn are only other white people—the eccentric wizards who come across as less than "respectable", the batty old spinster down the street who lives with cats.

My problem with *Harry Potter* is this. The first three or four books into the series, we fanfic speculators had observed that there were far too many children in this world and too few adults—what did all the kids graduating from Hogwarts every year do afterwards? There could only be so many Ministry of

2 Acknowledged by the *Daily Mail*, the newspaper Uncle Vernon favors. If you add the other non-white minorities, that takes it up 14 per cent, says James Chapman in "Ethnic minorities 'will make up one third of the population by 2050' as Britain's melting pot continues to grow", 5 May 2014. Accessed from http://www.dailymail.co.uk/news/article-2620957/Ethnic-minorities-make-one-population-2050-Britains-melting-pot-continues-grow.html on 31 July 2016.

Magic employees, St. Mungo's employees, Hogwarts employees, professional Quidditch players, magical-creature tamers, *Daily Prophet* correspondents, Diagon Alley shop-owners, or isolated reclusive wizards, who lived in Muggle neighborhoods and never seemed to do much for a living. Were *all* wizards not employed in wizard occupations independently wealthy, or did some of them choose to get Muggle careers and live as Muggles, simply because there weren't that many magical jobs going around? Rowling tries to address this void by giving the main characters a nineteen-year jump in the epilogue of the series, so let's check which kids we saw grow up into the adult life—Harry, Ron and Hermione, obviously; all of Ron's siblings; Draco Malfoy; Luna Lovegood; Neville Longbottom. See a character of color on that list? I don't.

Angelina Johnson is the only character of color who finds mention on that list, and that's because George Weasley happened to marry her. The last I heard of George, he was running Weasleys' Wizard Wheezes. (Although he is somewhat significantly absent in *The Cursed Child*, so I don't even know any more.) Does anyone know why the extremely competitive ex-captain of the Gryffindor quidditch team has been happily serving as a hausfrau, while her white sister-in-law goes on to be a professional player, and then the editor of the sports section of the *Daily Prophet*? During a public appearance in 2007, Rowling had mentioned in one line—because that's all that deserves—that Cho Chang married a Muggle.[3] Tell me why, by now, I've stopped being surprised.

My problem with *Harry Potter* is *especially* this—even in *The Cursed Child*, the story with which Rowling is waging these noble race wars and collecting praise from liberal white people all over the Internet, in the text itself there isn't a single non-white character who's actually likeable or even substantial. George Weasley is absent altogether, his Weasleys' Wiz-

3 A report of this event can be found on the *Times-Picayune*, 18 October 2007. Accessed from http://blog.nola.com/living/2007/10/new_orleans_students_give_rowl.html on 31 July 2016.

ard Wheezes now mysteriously run singlehandedly by Ron, so there's no opportunity for Angelina to show up. The off-the-page Padma Patil, existing only in an alternate timeline, is a joke—not only for her stereotyping, but more so for her obvious function in the story as a vehemently undesirable alternative to Hermione. And of all the children in *The Cursed Child*, I did not find anyone more cursed than the off-the-page Panju Weasley, loaded with a name that *no Indian in history* has ever had, since it happens to be a somewhat derogatory diminutive for the Punjabi community.[4] If anyone named Panju Weasley can abstain from becoming a patricide, in the main timeline or any other, I don't see why others named Albus Severus Potter or Scorpius Malfoy presume to have a chip on their shoulder.[5]

Since Rowling forgets to tell us what the children of color in the original series became as adults (in the original timeline, seeing that now we have many), allow me to take you on a thought experiment. Let's take a look at the actors who played them in the movies—kids whom we have watched growing up, only a few years behind the characters they potrayed. The actor who played Harry Potter became a sex symbol even before the movies were completed; he starred in a highly successful West End production of *Equus*, followed by a string of moderately successful Hollywood movies. The actor who played

4 Another reader, Krupa Gohli, seems to have Googled and discovered that Panju is the name of a riverine island north of Mumbai, and expressed so in a *Buzzfeed* article titled "What The Hell Is A Panju?" And Other Questions I, A Brown Potterhead, Have For J.K. Rowling", 4 August 2016. Accessed from https://www.buzzfeed.com/krupagohil/harry-potter-and-the-casual-racism?utm_term=.st3ND4GgW#.ibj8oR3n5 on 7 August 2016. In all my visits to Mumbai, I've never heard of this island, so I'm really intrigued to learn why Rowling considered it an appropriate choice for Ron and Padma to name their child. Unless, *horror horror* she couldn't even be bothered enough for this character to run a simple Google search about "Indian male names"?
5 I am not the only person up in arms against Panju Weasley, because *all* of Rowling's South Asian readers are aghast. Earlier, when she got away with misusing Parvati and Padma in both the books and the movies, we had been uncomfortable but too young to express our discomfort in words. For a taste of what others are saying, check out "Potterverse and its disservice to the South Asian community ('Panju' Weasley? Really?)" by Shivani Patel, *Hypable*, 3 August 2016. Accessed from http://www.hypable.com/panju-weasley-cursed-child/ on 5 August 2016.

Cedric Diggory went on to play a sparkling vampire in the *Twilight* movies, a part that has probably surpassed his *Harry Potter* role in popularity. The actor who played Hermione Granger, creepily enough, became a sex symbol younger than everyone else. In subsequent years, she modeled for Burberry; starred in the highly acclaimed movie *The Perks of Being a Wallflower*; and currently serves as a UN Women Goodwill Ambassador—one of the most easily recognizable celebrity feminists of our time. The actor who played Padma Patil was beaten up by the men of her family for having a non-Muslim boyfriend, called a prostitute, and nearly smuggled back into Bangladesh for an arranged marriage.[6]

One more time. Let's compare the careers of Emma Watson, whose real life is a close parallel to Hermione Granger's, and Noma Dumezweni, whose isn't. Watson—daughter of white lawyers (Hermione is a daughter of dentists); educated at an elite private school in Oxford (Hermione is educated at Hogwarts); a hockey player since childhood (breaking female stereotypes, just as Hermione did with her academic prowess); a social activist (just like Hermione with her Society for the Promotion of Elfish Welfare); undoubtedly encouraged by everyone whose opinion she *actually cares about* to feel as competent as any man. Compare to Dumezweni—daughter of black immigrants from Swaziland who escaped to the UK from the apartheid in South Africa; a non-native speaker of English; a single mother in her late forties; an actor highly skilled and barely known, despite the fact that she won the Laurence Olivier award a decade ago; someone who describes herself as "I'm a great company actor; a great supporting actor."[7]

6 A report of the assault on Afshan Azad can be found on the BBC website, titled understatedly "Harry Potter actress's brother jailed for attacking her", 21 January 2011. Accessed from http://www.bbc.com/news/uk-england-manchester-12248091 on 31 July 2016. A large part of the Harry Potter fandom never even heard this news, and many of those who did no longer remember it.
7 As reported by the *Guardian*, which featured an interview with Dumezweni after the *Cursed Child* casting was announced, 26 February 2016. Accessed from https://www.theguardian.

Spot the dissonance yet? The young Hermione Granger blended comfortably into the young Emma Watson, as did most of the white children in *Harry Potter* into the actors who played them, and that's the comfort all of us fans had come to associate with the *Harry Potter* franchise. The adult Emma Watson still *feels like* Hermione, with her feminism and her degree from Brown and her successful post-*Harry Potter* acting career. The person who decisively doesn't feel like Hermione—to me as well as to the racist readers—is Noma Dumezweni.

Rowling may have given Hermione frizzy hair and no particular skin color, but Hermione of the *Harry Potter* books is definitely not a black girl. She cannot be anything but white, not because Rowling *told us so*, but because Rowling managed to show-not-tell the hell out of that inevitability. The world of *Harry Potter* is a world where "tiny wizards run headlong through a wall at a busy London commuter station,"[8] just as it's a world where characters who are doubtlessly people of color always turn out to be inadequate when measured against their white peers, melt meekly into the background, or aren't even visible where they should be. Even colorblind texts sometimes just "happen to" show a person of color playing a more significant function than white people—*Twenty Thousand Leagues*, for instance; or every Hollywood movie with a non-white villain—but *Harry Potter* isn't one of those texts.

Consistency in worldbuilding does not only emerge over the laws of physics or which magical creature can do what; it is also felt through the unspoken patterns of social interaction between the characters, and the status quo they uphold.

---

com/stage/2016/feb/26/noma-dumezweni-hermione-harry-potter-and-the-cursed-child-palace-theatre on 31 July 2016.

8 As one more well-meaning, "incidentally" white, defendant of colorblindness, Grace Dent, points out in *The Independent*, 6 June 2016. Accessed from http://www.independent.co.uk/voices/if-you-think-noma-dumezweni-doesn-t-quite-fit-as-hermione-then-jk-rowling-is-right-you-re-racist-a7067726.html on 31 July 2016.

If you're trying to retcon a black Hermione into *Harry Potter*, you may as well throw in a few hobbits or sparkly vampires.

Or maybe you *can* retcon a black Hermione into *Harry Potter*, except that casting Noma Dumezweni in the play isn't what is called a retcon. Retcon—the device of altering already established events in the canon—is familiar enough to us from superhero comics, but there's a difference between a retcon and an unfaithful adaptation. A retcon introduces a retrospective change by offering a plausible (for a certain value of "plausible") explanation for why this change is not contradictory to the canon. If the change absolutely cannot be reconciled with the canon, the explanation often happens to be that the altered events took place in an alternate timeline that has no relationship with the original.

The Cursed Child abounds with retcons and alternate timelines, but in none of those is Hermione a black girl or woman. The existence of Delphini Diggory is a retcon; the existence of Panju Weasley is an alternate timeline. Hermione, however, is the same Hermione as before. She isn't black in the text of the play, just as she wasn't in the original books. There may be a later production of *The Cursed Child* in which Hermione is played by a white actor (although, having read the play, I cannot imagine why it would merit a later production), and all the "stains" of blackness will magically disappear.

So let's get this straight—the debate we're having here is not, in the first place, about Hermione being black, although Rowling and her supporters are also channeling it in that direction; but about a canonically white Hermione being played by a black actor. Having grown up in India, I don't find the idea of a character being played by an actor of a different race problematic in itself—all my life I've seen the works of Shakespeare or other English-language writers performed by fellow Indians, without assuming any race change in the original text. And most white people also don't find that idea problematic, *as long as* it's a white actor playing a character of any other race. When Noah Ringer plays Aang in *The Last Airbender* or Jake Gyllenhaal plays Dastan in *Prince of Persia*, no one assumes that the characters were rewritten as white.

In a truly colorblind world, no one would be talking about a black Hermione—because the Hermione of *Harry Potter* isn't and has never been black; she's Rowling's wishy-washy vision of a figure in a coloring book, one that can be filled in with any color you like. Except that figures that can be filled in with any color you like are essentially a white person's fantasy, because *they* are the ones who are allowed to play any of us any time they want. *We* aren't allowed to play them without changing the entire canonical description of the character into someone of our specific race; and that's the racist equation Rowling is feeding every time she defends her right of having written a black Hermione. She's completely unabashedly basking in the praise and diversity-friendly cred of having written a black protagonist without writing a single word of a black protagonist, merely agreeing to cast a black actor to play the character. Seriously, white-supremacy apologists, how many different kinds of wool do we need to be pulled over our eyes before it's finally enough?

On the other hand, the *Harry* Potter series—the "true" words of Rowling, as opposed to apocryphal fanfic speculation—had been my lifeline for years, and I can't bring myself to end this essay on a renouncing declaration, because I *know* I will be hanging around at Pottermore, muttering and cribbing. (Dare I bring up the analogy of how the "cursed" children feel about the parents who wish they were someone else? You created us, Rowling; sorry we didn't turn up like the fans you were primarily writing for. Sorry for being the wrong color. Sorry for managing to see the things in your stories that you refuse to acknowledge are there. Time for doing some Act-Four-Scene-Five-style soul-searching, maybe?)

So here's the thing—I'm angry and heartbroken with the way *Harry* Potter has turned out till now, but I will still lap it up gratefully if, in any of these further continuations of the series, the kids of color who weren't so cool at school *do* show up as successful and desirable adults. I'm sure Dumezweni is great, and everyone who has watched *The Cursed Child* enjoyed her performance, but I don't *want* this ridiculously see-through excuse of a black Hermione. I want an Angelina Johnson who gets to do cool things as an adult, and I want someone to cast Dumezweni or any other talented, underrated black actor to play her. I want Cho, Dean, Lee, Blaise or the Patil sisters to come back, and turn into *new* major characters.

I *want* the racists in my stories, and I want the racists to lose. I *want* people like the Dursleys to call people like me Paki, nigger, gangster, terrorist, job-stealer, the proverbial dogs that their country is going to, and then I want to see them eat their words. I want to see the Death Eaters swelling with ancestral wealth built over centuries of slavery and colonial- ism—because aren't they all old British aristocrats, and how else did those people get rich?—and mouthing their ancestral slurs. (Do you really think Draco Malfoy would've let Hermi- one off with just "Mudblood", if she happened to be black?) I don't want Mudblood to be a half-hearted allegory for gay, non-white or any other minority, I don't want house-elves to enact a half-baked allegory of slaves, because minorities are *not* allegorical in this world, they're *not* equal to the straight white people, and I'm sure Rowling knows that as well as I do.

So there, I have once again exercised my possessiveness about the *Harry Potter* canon to suggest to its author what she should do with it. My childhood letter addressed to Blooms- bury was never replied—I'm sure that was more because Rowling received thousands of such letters every day, and less because a little brown girl in Calcutta, India wasn't the default reader she was writing for, although I'm *also* sure that she was writing for all children. But *Harry Potter* had been a core part of my childhood, just as it was for any white child; and I hate to discover myself more and more rejected by it on each subsequent read. In the *Harry Potter* world a girl like me doesn't win, and I *want* to win, because I thought I was Hermione too. J.K. Rowling, this time are you listening?

One Girl in The Justice League

TANSY RAYNER
ROBERTS

I HAVE A PROBLEM WITH the "one girl" trope of superhero teams. It was a problem for me when the original Avengers movie only included Black Widow, and not the Wasp (who actually was the "one girl" founding member of the team). It's a problem for me now that the Justice League trailer (which I kind of loved) has been released into the world, with Wonder Woman clearly marked out as the only female character in the team.

This isn't me complaining about how super hero teams *should* look. I'm campaigning for realism based on a long, deep, fannish association with the Justice League.

But that's the thing about history—it often gets forgotten beneath the sinking weight of what people think history was like. That's why the word "tradition" has so much power.

In the 1960's Justice League comics, sure, there was one girl and that was Wonder Woman. In the early 1970's, when Wonder Woman left the Justice League and Black Canary joined up instead, there was one girl. In the mid 1980's, when the origin story of the Justice League was retweaked to diminish Wonder Woman's extensive history of one of DC's longest running and most iconic superheroes (I'm still angry about this), it was Black Canary and not Won-

143

der Woman who served as the original girl among the founding members.

In 1996 when Grant Morrison rebooted the Justice League, the front cover reflected that this super team had once more been restored to its 1960's original formula: six male super heroes and Wonder Woman. The same thing happened more or less with the New 52 reboot of Justice League in 2011.

And yet.

For the majority of the history of this long-running super team, it has actually been packed with women. Jam-packed. Black Canary might have taken over from Wonder Woman as the token girl during the Satellite Years in the 1970's, but the title already featured many recurring female superheroes including Zatanna (mistress of magic), Hawkgirl/Hawkwoman, and others. After Wonder Woman returned, there was more than a decade in which these four women were all active members of the Justice League alongside their male colleagues.

(Do you know who wasn't in the 1960's original team line up of the Justice League? Superman and Batman. The two of them refused to turn up to the first adventure because they were too busy and popular, and rarely bothered to check in with the team, except as occasional guest stars)

When the Justice League was rebooted as a teen-friendly book set in downtown Detroit in the mid 80's it featured 3 female heroes: Zatanna, Gypsy and Vixen, out of a team of 8.

When the Justice League was rebooted again in 1987, the main title included Japanese scientist/superhero Dr Light as well as Black Canary, and was soon split into two titles, Justice League International and Justice League Europe, the two teams including Fire, Ice, Big Barda, Huntress, Power Girl, Silver Sorceress, and Crimson Fox in their lineups. While the support team of JLI was male, the management and tech support that kept Justice League Europe running was done by Sue Dibny (wife of Elongated Man) and Catherine Colbert.

There were more reboots and reworkings of the Justice League titles throughout the 90's, with a fairly high turnover of creative teams behind the scenes as well as the casts of characters. Justice League Europe became Justice League International, the team including Dr Light, Crimson Fox (two different versions, with sisters taking turns in the costume), Power Girl and new Indian teenage superhero Maya. The former Justice League International became Justice League America, featuring Wonder Woman, Maxima, Fire and Ice. When Ice was killed in a massive Justice League crossover, the main Justice League America line brought back her "predecessor" Ice Maiden. Contradictions in the backstory of this character's former appearances were now explained as a separate character.

For almost its entire history, the norm for Justice League was to have at least two, but more commonly 3-4 women on each iteration of the team at all times. From the mid-80's onwards, it was normal to have at least one woman of colour and/or several women from non American origin per team, even when there were several different versions of the Justice League running concurrently. (Fire is Brazilian, Crimson Fox French, Ice Norwegian, Dr Light Japanese, Maya Indian, Power Girl from Atlantis, Vixen from Africa, Hawkgirl, Big Barda and Maxima alien, etc.)

In 1993 the titles were reshuffled again—Justice League Task Force contained only two recurring characters, the Martian Manhunter and Gypsy, but assembled a new crack team of Justice League members and affiliates for each mission—one of these, notably, was all female for plot reasons that also required the Martian Manhunter to shapeshift into a female body for several issues.

(This was handled with about as much sensitivity as you might expect for a mid-90's superhero comic).

Justice League Quarterly, an anthology series of short self-contained adventures, featured multiple all-female storylines, and many female characters. It also developed the backgrounds of affiliate characters and teams, such as Booster Gold's Conglomerate and the original Global Guardians, both of which also featured many, many female heroes.

Extreme Justice, the angry spiky shooty oh-so-nineties Justice League spin off, only featured one female member, Maxima, in its first issue but soon incorporated Plastique and Jayna of the Wonder Twins, with Carol Ferris as support.

Even Grant Morrison's massive "big guns" reboot which infuriated me at the time by resetting Justice League to an action comic instead of an adorable series of screwed up sitcom adventures, didn't keep Wonder Woman lonely as its "one girl" member for long. She was soon joined by Big Barda, Huntress, Oracle and Tomorrow Woman.

I lost touch with DC Comics after that. Possibly I was holding a grudge against Grant Morrison, and resentful that Fire and Blue Beetle weren't in comics any more. But Justice League kept on being brought back, and every time it did, it was full of women.

Justice League of America Vol 2 which came about after yet another Crisis event in 2006 featured Vixen, Hawkgirl, Black Canary, Wonder Woman. Later: Donna Troy, Starfire, Supergirl, Doctor Light, Jesse Quick.

Nostalgia for my beloved Justice League International built, at the same time that many of the characters from this era began to be killed off, retrospectively raped and/or generally treated badly by creative teams. Fans were treated to a few reunion titles, including Formerly Known As the Justice League (2003), I Can't Believe It's Not Justice

League (2005) and the rather darker and more intense Justice League: Generation Lost (2010).

Fire and Sue Dibny featured strongly in the 2003-2005 comedy titles, with Mary Marvel replacing the still-mourned, still-dead Ice as "the nice one" in counterpoint to Fire's brash energy. Power Girl was also included in I Can't Believe It's Not Justice League, and Ice herself made a reappearance—playing out an Orpheus/Eurydice storyline with Fire.

Ice was eventually brought back to life thanks to Gail Simone—her return was part of a Birds of Prey storyline. In 2010, Justice League: Generation Lost attempted to address some of the emotional fallout from the many horrible things that had happened to various former members of the JLI, with Fire and Ice's fractured friendship forming the heart of the story. Power Girl and Wonder Woman also had a prominent part in this story, which served as a retcon for Wonder Woman's out-of-character actions in the massive comics event 52.

This has all been about comics, but let's talk about the animated series! The very popular short run of the animated Justice League followed the long-running success of the Batman and Superman cartoons—and this version of the Justice League made 2 key changes to the "classic" line up, by featuring Hawkgirl as an original member of the team alongside Wonder Woman, and also by choosing the John Stewart (African American) version of Green Lantern to feature, instead of super-boring always-terrible hey-he-murdered-people Hal Jordan.

The follow up series, Justice League Unlimited, took a cue from the comics by featuring dozens and dozens of female teammembers in active adventures. Pretty much every woman I have mentioned so far in this history (and hey, there have been a lot of them) were included as part of the epic, rotating team.

Even the terriblawesome classic cartoon Super Friends from the 1970's brought in the Wonder Twins, Zan and Jaina, so that Wonder Woman wouldn't be the only girl on the team.

In 2011 there was another massive DC Comics reboot, The New 52—like Crisis of Infinite Earths in 1985 this affected the entire line and DC universe, rewriting backstories as well as retooling comic titles. The unfortunate effect of this particular reboot was to reset many classic characters to their "original" settings, throwing out decades of history, legacy and development of diversity. This love letter to the past was best embodied by the cover of the New 52's Justice League—featuring six men (Cyborg replacing the Martian Manhunter but otherwise the standard list: Superman, Batman, Aquaman, Hal Jordan's Green Lantern, Barry Allen's Flash) plus Wonder Woman.

As with the first issue of Grant Morrison's run, I wanted to punch a wall. Because WHY? Why is it that the default is always to this weird, unbalanced version of what a superhero team might look like, based on something that was thought up in the 1960's? Having a single female member is not remotely representative of the entire history of Justice League comics throughout their entire history, and yet. And yet.

The New 52 also featured an attempt at Justice League International, which was so awful I can't even tell you, BUT it featured Vixen, Fire, Ice and former Global Guardian Godiva. Of course, it killed off, sidelined and/or brutally injured most of the women in the first couple of issues, but even this TRULY AWFUL and HIGHLY DISAPPOINTING version of the Justice League still managed to put four female heroes into its team.

DC Comics and Justice League slipped away from me after that, the New 52 killing off a great deal of my interest and trust. But I will note that Justice League of America Vol. 3 starting from 2012 included Amanda Waller, Katana, Catwoman, Star Girl, Supergirl.

The most recent reboot of DC Comics is happening right now—DC Rebirth is attempting yet again to convince readers that this time things will be less complicated. Here's this for progress: the cover of DC Rebirth Justice League #1 features two female superheroes, because it finally occured to them that you can have a female Green Lantern. That's progress!

There is no excuse and no reason why a 21st century superhero team should not feature multiple female team members, whether we are talking about comics or TV shows or movies. This is every bit as true for the Justice League as it was for the Avengers. It doesn't matter who turned up the first adventure back in 1960—hell, that origin story of the Justice League has been rewritten and retold so many times in the comics, it's unrecognis-able. Sometimes they don't even include Starro the Conqueror!

The casting and reshaping of characters like Aquaman and the Flash to be very different from their 60's origins makes it clear that the makers of these movies are fine with taking as many liberties as they like with history to make a story that resonates with modern day audiences. That part is good. That's how it should be. History should be a starting point, not a weight around your neck.

Shaping a Justice League movie with only "one girl" in the story is a creative choice they made now, not a tradition that anyone was going to hold them to. Zack Snyder and his team made that choice, just as the DC bosses made that choice in 2011 and in 1996, and in 1960. They made that choice because having one woman on a team full of supermen looks right to them. It feels right. It feels like that's the way the history of superheroes and super teams is supposed to look. It feels "iconic."

Do you know what my Justice League movie would look like?

TANSY'S JUSTICE LEAGUE MOVIE

It would have Wonder Woman (Gal Gadot) teaming up with Oracle (Alia Shawkat) to find the World's Greatest Heroes, because there's an alien invasion coming, and she's going to need a team at her back. (Yes, Starro the Conqueror is coming, shut up, it's TRADITION)

She would gather her troops:

Black Canary (Kate McKinnon) has retired as a martial artist vigilante and is running her mother's florist but she hates plants and jumps at any excuse to get back into action.

Zatanna (Parminder Nagra) is about to go on stage for her Las Vegas stage extravaganza, but when Diana calls she's willing to send her understudy on stage, with the help of some real magical illusions.

Wonder Woman finds Vixen (Gina Torres) in Africa, Power Girl (Katee Sackhoff) in Atlantis, Hawkwoman (Aubrey Plaza) in Egypt.

Doctor Light (Lucy Liu) has students to teach, a paper to write and several experiments on the boil but yes, fine, for you Diana...

Fire (Mila Kunis) has been trying to convince Ice (Tuppence Middleton) to use her superpowers to fight crime for years, and now she finally has an excuse!

It's like *Ocean's 11* but with better dialogue, superpowers and telepathic starfish trying to take over the world! Hell, let's throw Margot Robbie's Harley Quinn in there, she'd be great!

Batman will appear in a single scene, explaining to Wonder Woman why gathering so many superheroes in one place is a dream that will never work. He can be Starro the Conqueror's first victim.

This movie wouldn't be called *Justice League Bomb-*

shells, or *Justice League Ame-Comi*, or *Justice League Ladies*. It would be called *Justice League*, because every one of the heroes I mentioned is just as important to the history of the Justice League as Batman or Barry Allen or Aquaman.

Oh, Blue Beetle would be in the movie too. To provide tech for the team, and to banter with Oracle. Because, you know. Gotta have a dude.

About the Contributors

ISABEL YAP writes fiction and poetry, works in the tech industry, and drinks tea. Born and raised in Manila, she has also lived in California, Tokyo, and London. In 2013 she attended the Clarion Writers Workshop. Her work has recently appeared on Tor.com, *Uncanny Magazine*, *Shimmer Magazine*, and *Year's Best Weird Fiction volume 2*. *Hurricane Heels*, her short fiction series about magical girls, is forthcoming from Book Smugglers Publishing. She is @visyap on Twitter and her website is isabelyap.com.

SUSAN JANE BIGELOW is a fiction writer, political columnist, and librarian. She mainly writes science fiction and fantasy novels. Her short fiction has appeared in *Strange Horizons*, *Apex Magazine*, *Lightspeed Magazine*'s "Queers Destroy Science Fiction" issue, and the Lamba Award-winning "The Collection: Short Fiction from the Transgender Vanguard," among others. She lives with her wife in northern Connecticut, and is probably currently at the bottom of a pile of cats. Visit her website The Extrahuman Union.

Though best known as one of the Emmy Award-winning producers of *Lost*, and for creating *The Middleman* comic books and TV series, **JAVIER GRILLO-MARXUACH** is a prolific creator of TV, films, graphic novels, and trans-media content. In addition to his work as writer/producer on shows ranging from *The 100*, and *The Shannara Chronicles*, to *Medium*, and *Boomtown*, Grillo-Marxuach co-hosts the *Children of Tendu* podcast, an educational series for writers, and is an avid participant of the Writers Guild mentors program. Grillo-Marxuach can be found online at OKBJGM.com, on twitter

@OKBJGM, and his podcast is available free of charge on iTunes, Stitcher, and at ChildrenOfTendu.com. Javier Grillo-Marxuach was born in San Juan, Puerto Rico, and his name is pronounced "HA-VEE-AIR-GREE-JOE-MARKS-WATCH".

MICHAL WOJCIK was born in Poland, raised in the Yukon Territory, and educated in Edmonton and Montreal. He has a Master's degree in history from McGill University, where he studied witchcraft trials in early modern Poland. His short fiction has appeared in *On Spec: The Canadian Magazine of the Fantastic*, *Clockwork Canada* and Pornokitsch. Follow him on his blog, onelastsketch. wordpress.com.

KATE ELLIOTT is the author of twenty-six fantasy and science fiction novels, including her New York Times bestselling YA fantasy, *Court of Fives* (and its sequel, *Poisoned Blade*) Her most recent epic fantasy is *Black Wolves*, and she's also written *Cold Magic* (first volume of the Spiritwalker Trilogy), an Afro-Celtic post-Roman gaslamp fantasy adventure with well-dressed men, bad ass women, and lawyer dinosaurs. Other series include the Crossroads Trilogy, the seven-volume Crown of Stars epic fantasy, the sf Novels of the Jaran, and a short fiction collection, *The Very Best of Kate Elliott*. Born in Iowa and raised in farm country in Oregon, she currently lives in Hawaii, where she paddles outrigger canoes for fun and exercise. You can find her on Twitter at @KateElliottSFF.

JIM ZUB is a writer, artist and art instructor based in Toronto, Canada. Over the past fifteen years he's worked for a diverse array of publishing, movie and video game clients including Marvel, DC Comics, Capcom, Hasbro, Cartoon Network, and Bandai-Namco. He juggles his time between being a freelance comic writer and Program Coordinator for Seneca College's award-winning Animation program. His current comic projects include *Dungeons & Dragons*, a new series celebrating 40 years of the classic tabletop RPG, *Thunderbolts*, the return of Marvel's villainous superhero team, and *Wayward*, a modern supernatural story about teens fighting Japanese mythological monsters.

ANNA HIGHT currently lives in Easthampton, MA, with a big white cat named Marvin. She plays a lot of Dungeons & Dragons and reads a lot of fanfiction. She wrote her first book at the age of ten, about a family of snakes, and her mother really liked it. "Ruby" is her first published short story.

SEANAN MCGUIRE lives, writes, and falls into blackberry brambles in the Pacific Northwest. She is the heart of every corn maze and the last piece of candy in the pillowcase, and she believes that Halloween is every day. Seanan can be found at www.seananmcguire.com, and probably needs a nap.

YOON HA LEE's space opera *Ninefox Gambit*, the first in a trilogy from Solaris Books, came out in 2016. His collection *Conservation of Shadows* was published by Prime Books in 2013, and his short fiction has appeared in Tor.com, *The Magazine of Fantasy & Science Fiction*, *Lightspeed*, *Clarkesworld*, *Beneath Ceaseless Skies*, *Uncanny Magazine*, and other venues. He lives in Louisiana with his family and an extremely lazy cat, and has not yet been brave enough to cook gator.

YUKIMI OGAWA lives in a small town in Tokyo, where she writes in English but never speaks the language. She still wonders why it works that way. Her fiction has appeared in such places as *Fantasy & Science Fiction*, *Strange Horizons*, and *Lackington's*.

MIMI MONDAL lives between Calcutta, India and Philadelphia, PA. She has been an editor at Penguin India; a Commonwealth Scholar in Scotland; and an Octavia Butler Scholar at the Clarion West Writing Workshop. Her first collection, *Other People*, is scheduled to be published in India from Juggernaut Books.

TANSY RAYNER ROBERTS lives in Tasmania, Australia with her partner and two daughters. She has written and edited various science fiction and fantasy books including the Mocklore Chronicles, the Creature Court trilogy, *Love & Romanpunk* (a short story suite) and *Cranky Ladies of History*. She is the host or co-host of three podcasts: Galactic Suburbia, Verity! and Sheep Might Fly, and has won two Hugo Awards, for Best Fan Writer and Best Fancast. You can find Tansy on Twitter (@tansyrr) and at her blog tansyrr. com which features fiction, feminist essays, comics reviews and pop culture criticism.

KRISTINA TSENOVA was born in 1995 in Bulgaria and is currently a student at Glasgow Caledonian University. Her preferred media is watercolor, acrylic and digital painting. She has had two exhibitions in 2014 and has won approx. 50 art competitions. Apart from traditional art, her interests include cinematography, literature and photography. She is also a hobbyist photographer and makes short movie clips and in the future, she would like to work on varied design projects, concept art and special effects for the movie industry. A great source of inspiration are the movies of Hayao Miyazaki and the genuine art of Pascal Campion. You can find her on deviantart and on facebook.

ANA GRILO is a Brazillian who moved to the UK because of the weather. No, seriously. She works with translations in RL and hopes one day The Book Smugglers will be her day job. When she's not at The Book Smugglers, or hogging the twitter feed, she can be found blogging over at Kirkus with Thea or podcasting with Renay at Fangirl Happy Hour.

THEA JAMES oversees digital marketing and strategy at a major publishing house by day. She is also half of the maniacal book review duo behind The Book Smugglers, a Hugo Award nominated speculative fiction book review blog and publisher of short stories, novellas, novels, and genre-focused nonfiction.

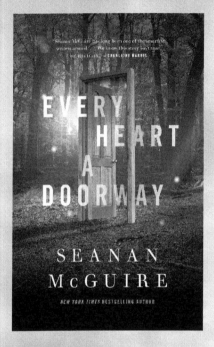

Made in the USA
Charleston, SC
08 December 2016